CW00985439

BOY NEXT DOOR

Raquel Lyon is an English author, who writes YA fantasy and NA contemporary romance stories. Her heroines are kinda kooky, her heroes slightly devilish, and her romance a bit on the raunchy side. If the sun is out, so is she. She has a crazy sugar addiction and eats ice cubes as if they're going out of fashion.

To hear about new releases, join Raquel's mailing list: http://eepurl.com/tuKUv

Follow on twitter @raquel_lyon or on facebook at www.facebook.com/raquellyon.

Also available:

BOY NEXT

RAQUEL LYON

Copyright 2014 All right reserved

Createspace Edition

978-1500357627

First Edition

This book is sold subject to the condition that it may not be lent, re-sold, hired out, or otherwise circulated in any form other than that in which it is published.

Thank you for respecting the hard work of the author.

♠ ♠ ♠

Chapter One

Three years. Three years of partying with dirty fingernails. Three years to get a degree in how to dig a hole and stick something in it. It doesn't take a genius to do that, but it does require a piece of paper to let future employers know that you can. I'm about to get that piece of paper, so I should be stoked, ready to move up in the world, or at least stick my size elevens into it. Instead, I'm back where I started, Pappa's house. As much as I loved the old place, I never thought I'd have to call it home.

Dumping my worldly possessions onto the perfectly varnished slats of the front porch of number twenty-three Parkside Avenue, I freed up my hands to open the door.

"Pappa! Paps, I made it." Smokey, Pappa's ageing Retriever, bounded towards me, his tail wagging furiously. "Hey, boy. Where's the old man, asleep again?" I asked, bending my knees to pet him and receiving a dog-dribble face in response.

Despite entering his seventy-sixth year, Ronald Kempton, kept his home perfectly, right down to the blue and white urn, holding my grandmother's ashes, sitting pride of place on the mantelpiece, and looking around the pristinely decorated living room, filled with antique furniture, brought back many childhood memories, every one of them sad since my parents had joined Nan in the big unknown. In the corner, Pappa's favourite armchair was empty. I wasn't surprised; afternoon naptime was over.

I dragged my bags over the porch and into the hallway. Smokey sniffed them excitedly. He clearly had a thing for the scent of dirt and fertiliser, although how he could detect any smell other than Pappa's pipe tobacco amazed me. The scent hung in the air like thick city smog, meaning the old man couldn't be far away.

Smokey followed me as I strode through to the kitchen and headed for the patio doors. Second only to Pappa's love for his armchair was his love of the garden, and I fully expected to find him there. I wasn't wrong. The familiar curve of Argyle sweater stooped over an impressive row of cabbages, pulling out stray weeds.

"You should be kneeling down to do that. You'll put your back out again," I said with a mixture of chastisement and endearment.

Pappa's receding hairline rotated to face me. "Johnny! Hello, son. I wasn't expecting you until four."

"It's ten past, Paps."

"Is it? Well, well. How time flies. I'll just get these last few strays, and then I'll help you settle in."

Squatting down next to him, I said, "Let me give you a hand, and then maybe you'll be qualified to write me a reference when I start job hunting." It was an icebreaker not a serious request.

"I doubt your grandfather giving a glowing account of your weed pulling prowess would cut much mustard." He chuckled and slapped my back, warm-heartedly. "It's good to have you home."

Home. Over the past decade, I hadn't spent more than a few hours between these walls, and yet home was what it was now. Since Dad downed a bunch of painkillers—six months after Mum failed to wake up from the operating table—Pappa was all the family my brother and I had left.

I threw one last green shoot into the waiting bucket and assisted Pappa to his feet.

"I hope you like steak," he said. "I got us a couple of rumps for tonight. A sort of welcome home celebration."

"Great. But only a couple? Is Kendrick eating out?" I asked, as we crossed the lawn towards the house.

"Your guess is as good as mine, son. Pleases himself, that boy. I never know whether he's in or out." Pappa stopped to tip the weeds into the garden bin. "Maybe I'm too old for this parenting lark, or perhaps I was blessed with a well-behaved daughter, but Kendrick trawls in at all hours of the night with no explanation as to where he's been."

"Teenagers tend to do that, Paps."

"Yes, I appreciate that. I may be ready for my wooden overcoat, but I haven't forgotten what it's like to be young. Still, I worry about what he gets up to, and I suspect he's missing college too. I was hoping you could have a word." He shook the bucket empty and discarded it next to the shed. "Steer him in the right direction, you know. He looks up to you."

I waited patiently for him to finish tidying up. "Sure thing."

Over the fence, the sound of someone else putting out the trash caught my curiosity, and I strained my neck to peer through a gap in the lilac bush. The blonde-haired woman turned to return to her house before I managed to see her face, but my eyes followed her tight, little ass all the way to the doorstep, and I felt a familiar stirring in my jeans. A great ass got to me every time.

Pappa noticed my scrutiny. "I don't think you've ever met Cora, have you? She moved here a few years ago. Lovely woman. Single too. If only I were thirty years younger." He chuckled. "Her daughters are a chip off the old block, too. They must be about your age, now. You could do worse," he said, entering the kitchen.

—

"Yeah?" I'd spent the past few months concentrating on getting through my exams, relying on the old one-handed mambo to keep me company at night, so if any half-sexy momma could get my juices flowing, I figured it was time to get back out there and find myself a girl. It couldn't hurt to check out the daughters. "Good to know."

Pappa cooked a mean steak, and with a fully satisfied stomach, I set about unpacking.

My room was the smallest one in the house—a case of last one in gets the cupboard, I reckoned—but I didn't mind. It had once belonged to my mother, and I could almost feel her essence lingering in the faded wallpaper, as if she were somehow looking out for me. As far back as I could remember, the room had remained unaltered. In fact, I'd been born on the very bed still squished under the window, as it had been for the last twenty-two years. Even the purple candlewick bedspread had survived the decades, and there was barely enough floor space to dump my bags on the moth-eaten carpet, due to the oppressive dark wooden wardrobe dominating the remaining space. If I did manage to bag myself a woman, no way would I be bringing her back here. A shag palace it wasn't. A girl would have to be one card short of a full deck to find my new digs a turn on. The sooner I could set myself up with a set of wheels the better.

After stuffing the last of my T-shirts into a drawer in the base of the mahogany mountain, I tossed my holdall onto its top, as footsteps clumped up the stairs.

The door flew open.

"Hey, Bro. Welcome to God's waiting room." My brother leaned against the doorjamb, a cigarette dangling from the corner of his mouth.

"Since when did you start smoking?"

"You haven't seen me for nearly a year, and I get a fucking lecture for a hello?"

Dressed all in black in a cut-off T-shirt and ripped jeans, Kendrick had certainly altered in that time. When I'd returned to uni, last year, he'd been into computer games, cars, and very little else, with ambitions of becoming a mechanic, and it had always been my plan to buy a plot of land, where he could run his garage business alongside my gardening one.

"Pappa hinted you'd gone off the rails. I can see what he means."

"He doesn't get me."

"He's cool for an old guy."

"Yeah, real old. Kinda kills the street cred dossing with a wrinkly. Town's okay, though. I can fill you in on some decent hangouts. Fancy shooting some pool tonight?"

"I had planned to get my head down soon. Bit knackered after that long journey."

"Didn't you kip on the train?"

"Well, yeah, but ..."

"You're good then. You can sleep some more when you're dead."

It was pointless trying to reason with my brother. When he made his mind up, he was as stubborn as they came, and I had no energy to start off our reconciliation with an argument, so resigned to getting my ass whipped at pool, I grabbed my wallet and keys and shoved them into the pocket of my jeans, on the way out. With a bit of luck, Kendrick would tire of beating me after a couple of rounds, and I'd be able to slip away early.

As we exited the front door, a woman jogged along the pavement. Kendrick's eyes followed her and he let out a wolf whistle. The woman's blonde ponytail swished rhythmically above her figure-hugging outfit: black with pink sections at the side to give the appearance of a smaller waist. Not that she needed any assistance in that area. She had a damn fine figure, and there was something familiar about the line of her Lycra covered ass. Without breaking her stride or casting a sideways glance, she continued up the neighbouring driveway.

Kendrick angled his head and watched her all the way into the house. "Fucking smoking, man, that one. I swear if

I ever get the itch to tap a MILF, she's top of my list. Pert ass and tits that still point in the right direction, mm-mm."

"Was that Cora?" I asked, thinking her front was as sweet as her rear.

"I didn't know you knew her?"

"I don't. She was in her back yard, earlier. Paps mentioned her name," I commented casually, as we walked off in the opposite direction, and I snuck a backward glance on the off chance she'd re-emerged.

"He would. I think the old dog has a soft spot for her. Lecherous old bastard." He lit another cigarette and snapped his Zippo shut. "I bet he mentioned the daughters, too, didn't he?"

I nodded. "Ah-huh. I think he was playing matchmaker. What do you reckon? Worth the bother?"

"Nah, dude. Fucking hot, granted, but stuck-up."

"You mean you struck out." I thumped his shoulder playfully. Despite his talk, I doubted that, at seventeen, my brother had the right skills to pull the babes.

Kendrick's arm wrapped around my neck and he pretended to punch my head in return. "Me strike out? Never. This town's ripe with easy tail. One look at those two and you can tell, high maintenance, the pair of them. Why bother with the hassle?" He let me go and resumed walking. "Besides, I think they're both hooked up."

That'd be right. "You got a girl, then?"

"I like to keep my options open."

I stuck my hands in my pockets, and we rounded a corner onto the main street. "I'll take that as a no."

"I do all right." He winked. "What about you? Get much action in the old geek shack?"

"I did all right," I answered, mirroring his brush-off.

The last time I'd walked down Tirdle Road, I was holding my mum's hand, with Nanna pushing Kendrick in his pram, on our way to the park. Of course, that was before Mum became ill. After that, a visit to our grandparent's house resulted in nothing more than kicking a ball around the back garden or a game of Scrabble, if it rained. But the street was much as I remembered it, filled with dark buildings housing too many fast-food takeaways and taxicab offices. Nothing changed.

After a few more steps, Kendrick stopped. "We're here," he said.

Nestled in a red brick wall, a black door faded into the shadows. Above it the neon sign glowed with the words Pocket Scratcher.

My eyebrows rose at the name. "You sure this is the right place?"

"You think I got lost in the two hundred yards we just walked? I come here all the time."

"Sounds like a gay club."

"Anything but, Bro, anything but." He slapped me on the shoulder and steered me inside. "Mind you, if you're into that kind of thing, I know a few joints. Great places to pick up the chicks. It's surprising how many of them are up for proving they can straighten you out." His eyebrows shot up. "Gotta admit, I've let a few of them think they have."

I laughed, undecided as to whether I believed him or not. "Maybe next time."

Inside the club, the smoky atmosphere hit me like a gas cloud. Had they not heard of the smoking ban? "Christ, does anyone ever get out of here alive?" I asked.

"You'll get used to it," Kendrick said. "Pete, the owner, has chain smoked for years. Doesn't give a damn about the penalties. He's cool. It's one of the reasons it's so popular here." He lifted a Doc Marten onto the metal footrest and leaned over the bar. "That and the back room poker."

My interest piqued. Kendrick had no idea what an intriguing snippet of information he'd revealed. Poker was rife at uni, and I'd learned fast. Not only had my winnings provided beer money, but I'd stashed a good amount in the bank too. Mum's life insurance had taken care of my student loans, and there was even a bit left over. I figured with a few years of hard graft, I'd have enough to buy the patch of land, before I reached thirty. But if I could get a few games in here, perhaps I could reach my goal sooner than I thought. "Ever been in?"

"Where?"

"The back room."

"Couple of times. Lucked out, though. There're some serious dudes in there, Bro. And serious consequences for those who don't pay up. Got my nose busted open for owing a twenty. You play poker?"

"Doesn't everyone? Can you get me in?"

"Invite only."

Figured as much. "So, who did you have to shag?"

"Fuck off. Everyone loves me here." The barman slammed two bottles of beer in front of us and snatched the waiting note. Rick picked up his bottle and nodded at the other. "Grab that and rack 'em up."

Chapter Two

Three beers and two games later, we were in the middle of the decider.

"Hey there, sexy." A girl, with more flesh on show than she had covered, sidled up to Kendrick. Her long, black hair flowed in waves down her bare back, stopping short of her hip hugging skirt. She wrapped her arms around his waist and planted a more than friendly kiss on his cheek.

"Hey yourself," Kendrick replied. "I thought you were grounded. Did you get time off for good behaviour?"

"Me, good behaviour? Get real. I snuck out."

"Lucky me." His eyes drank in the girl's cleavage as he talked. "You here for some action?"

I could spot a slut at ten paces, and I leaned back against the pool table, watching, as she trailed a finger down Kendrick's chest. Evidently I'd been wrong about his skills, even if he had hooked up with a tramp. The way she draped her body over his did more than suggest she was a regular fuck-buddy, and even though alley catting isn't my scene, I had to admire his style.

"I could be, but I'm here with Tina. She's at the bar getting the drinks in," she said.

"And if I sort Tina out?"

"I am *not* sharing you."

"Actually, I was talking about my brother, newly back from uni and looking for company." Great, Bro. Thanks for labelling me a loser who can't pick up his own skirt.

"Brother? I didn't know you had a brother, Rick."

Kendrick cocked his chin in my direction. "Johnny, meet Lexi. Lexi, Johnny."

I held up a palm in silent greeting.

Lexi angled her head and ran the tip of her tongue over her teeth. "Hmm. I might be willing to re-think the sharing thing on my part. I see your family went halves on the good looks."

Kendrick slapped her butt cheek. "You really are a little slut, aren't you?"

"Oh, baby." Lexi pouted. "Have I hurt your feelings? I didn't realise you wanted exclusivity."

"You haven't. And I don't." He pulled her closer and they locked lips.

Tina arrived with the drinks, walking past me without a glance. She nudged one at Lexi. "Jeez, Lex. I thought we'd come for a quick game. Don't say you're leaving me hanging again?" She stood tapping her foot until the couple broke contact.

"Course not," Lexi said, accepting her drink. "You can have a booty call too. Rick has a brother." She looked over Tina's shoulder and smiled at me.

I studied my potential date. Not conventionally pretty, and certainly not my usual type, this girl was all skin and bone, long and lean, no curves at all. Only her fluffy, fake fur jacket, prevented her looking like a stick stuck into black, scuffed stilettos.

Her red hair flew out, like a flag blowing at the top of a flagpole, as she swung around to greet me. "Hi, Rick's brother. How's it hanging?" she asked, her gaze travelling down to my jeans, and spending a moment too long there, before reverting to my face.

"Can't complain."

As she downed half of her drink in one long mouthful, I found myself wondering what else she could fit in that wide mouth. Yeah, it was definitely time to get laid by an actual woman again. I'd almost forgotten what one felt like. It wasn't as if I'd climbed on the leg-over wagon, but after one too many one-night stands, at uni, I'd realised that getting off for a few minutes, or an hour, relieves the frustrations but gains no lasting satisfaction. Sleeping around just wasn't my scene. It was time to find that elusive, meaningful love: the kind my parents shared, the destructive kind that ends badly more often than it works out. I was ready. I wanted it. Tina wasn't it. But it didn't hurt to take what was on offer, and Tina was definitely offering. One last random shag could be just what I needed. The game was a bust anyway. Kendrick had Lexi up against the wall, greedily partaking of every inch of her exposed caramel flesh.

Tina inched closer. "So, where you been hiding, then?"

"Uni."

"Brainbox, huh? That mean you're gonna get one of those city toff jobs and earn loads of dosh?" She threw her head back, laughing, like one of those boxed clowns at the funfair: a horsey laugh with little snorts at the end.

"Nah, not my style, babe."

She raised a sceptical brow, finished her drink, and lit a cigarette. Was I the only one who didn't smoke around here? "You wanna go somewhere?" she asked, chewing on a piece of gum like a cow chewing cud.

"Like where?"

"Anywhere. You choose."

"How about your place?"

"Still live with my folks and three baby sisters." She paused for a second. "Guys usually wanna go to Crown Point."

Yeah, I bet. "I don't have wheels yet."

"Your house?"

It was past midnight, and Pappa's hearing wasn't what it used to be. I pictured him snoring heavily in his bed. We might get away with the sofa, if she was quiet. It was worth a shot, and better than taking her up against the side alley wall surrounded by discarded kebab trays and yesterday's empty beer bottles.

"I'm bunking with my grandfather. I guess it would be okay. But no screaming."

Her eyes twinkled. "You usually make girls scream?"

"Don't get too excited. You want something. I want something. I'm not out to impress."

Tina shrugged; clearly not out to impress me, either.

Arriving at the end of Pappa's driveway, I was puzzled to see the living room light still glowing. Didn't all old folk crash early? Perhaps he'd left on the bulb as a welcome home, or fallen asleep in his chair.

"Wait here," I whispered.

I crept up to the window and peered through a gap in the curtains. The standard lamp lit up Pappa's spot, and there he was, newspaper and pen in hand, scribbling away. Shit. Who does a fucking crossword in the middle of the night? I contemplated sneaking Tina past him and up to my room, but there was always the chance he might see, and this girl wasn't worth upsetting Paps for. I turned to Tina. "The old man's still awake. Some other time, maybe."

"Not so fast, buster. Don't you know it's bad form to get a girl all worked up and drop her without so much as a fumble? What about the garage?"

Fuck me. She was desperate to get some. "It's locked, and I don't have a key."

"Round the back then?"

I thought for a moment. "There's a shed."

"Perfect."

A few minutes later, I had Tina pressed up against the wooden slats next to the plant pots. She had her hand up my shirt, running those huge lips over my stomach faster than a whip crack, and I had to admit, it felt kinda good. Wet, but good. In the dark, I tried to put another face to my date, but the only one I could conjure up was Cora's. A bevy of beauties out there, and all that came to mind was somebody's frigging mother. I pulled Tina's head level with mine and kissed her hard, imagining her friend Lexi instead. At least Lexi was young and pretty. I wouldn't have minded going there for the night, if Kendrick hadn't staked his claim first. Tina responded with enthusiasm, prising my lips open with her tongue and thrusting inside. She tasted of cigarettes. Old, musty cigarettes. I imagined it must be a similar experience to lick a dirty ashtray. Not that I'd ever tried it, even in my most drunken of moments. Tina's mouth was as big as her lips suggested, and I struggled to keep up with it. An episode of tonsil tennis was normally all it took to get me geared up for the main action, and yet, things were oddly quiet down there. My dick obviously found Tina as unattractive as my eyes did. It was time to get things moving.

Raising my hands from her waist, I headed for her tits, but they were so flat, it felt like I was touching up a freaking boy. She let out a moan. She liked it. Me, not so much. Even thumbing her nipples brought no response where it was needed. This was gonna be a tough call. I couldn't have her opening that big mouth of hers and spreading it around town that I couldn't get it up.

Her hands moved further under my T-shirt, pushing it up until I let her slip it over my head. Then her lips smoothed over my pecs, and she fumbled with my fly, opening it and pushing my jeans past my hips. My dick flopped into her hand.

"You're not ready." She sounded disappointed.

I shrugged. "Probably the beer."

"Hmm." She glanced up for a second before looking down again. "Let's see if we can get things moving, shall we?" Her fingers set to work, and my blood pumped. "Must be wearing off," she said. "It's stiffening."

Couldn't she just shut the fuck up? I was finally gaining traction, but her voice was killing the mood. I pushed on her shoulders, and she got the message.

Yeah, that's right, rubber lips, down you go. Ahh.

Thankfully, that mouth was good for something after all, and I was hard in seconds. Thinking about Cora's ass in her skintight shorts helped. What was it about that woman? Pappa and Kendrick had both succumbed to her charms and now she was wheedling her way under my skin too. But hell, at least something was working, and I'd take what I could get.

"I think that's done the trick," she said with a note of satisfaction. "My turn."

What the fuck? If she thought I was going down on her, she could forget it. My tongue was not going to the same place I imagined dozens of dicks in town had. I grabbed her by the shoulders and flipped her around to bend over the potting bench.

"Whoa there. Not so rough," she protested.

"Sorry." I reached under her skirt and yanked down her panties. I needed to get the job done before she softened my wood with her voice.

With one hand on her bare ass, I rooted for my wallet with the other.

"Hurry up," Tina shouted.

"Can you just be quiet for one damn minute? I'm trying to find a rubber." I always kept one on me, just in case. I prayed it wasn't out of date.

"I'm on the pill."

"Good for you." Girls lied about that kind of thing. I knew. My best buddy at uni had been caught out like that, and I'd be damned if I was going to let it happen to me.

Besides, when you go swimming with sharks, you need a strong cage.

When I thrust into her, she gasped, and her nails scraped over the tabletop, but she bent her knees and rocked against me, encouraging a faster rhythm. Tina could fuck. Bonus. Steadying the pace, I focused on building to release, feeling bad that I didn't fancy the girl, but hey, she was getting what she wanted, just as much as I was. Trouble was, as I rammed harder, and the pressure built, my thoughts were honed on one thing. Cora's ass.

Chapter Three

It was almost lunchtime when I crawled out from under the bedspread and moseyed down to the kitchen. I poured a glass of juice and gazed through the window as I drank. The sun was out, and Pappa was pruning the hedge, with Smokey laid out at his feet, black fur shimmering in the breeze. I went outside to say good morning.

When he saw me, Smokey wagged his tail, jumped up, and ran around my legs. I stroked his back as I asked, "Need a hand, Paps?"

"Oh, morning, son." Pappa looked flushed and was panting from the exertion. "It would be wonderful if you could save me stretching. Grab those ladders over there and start on the top, if you would. There's another pair of shears in the shed, at least there should be. I was actually in two minds about whether to call the police or not. The shed appears to have been broken into, last night."

Yeah, by a horny couple. "What makes you say that?" I asked, opening the shed door.

"Stuff everywhere, tools on the floor which I know I hung up, broken plant pots, and they made a right mess of my potting bench. Haven't found anything missing, though. Very strange."

I scanned the shed quickly for the shears, noting the gouges along the table's surface. Tina had had sharp nails. "Most likely kids," I shouted.

"All the same, I think I'll run down to the hardware store this afternoon and buy a padlock. I've been meaning to fix one on for ages," he replied.

Finding the shears, I tucked them into my back pocket, and picked up the ladders on my way back. "I can do that for you, Paps. I've had some flyers made, advertising my gardening services. They might let me leave a few on the counter."

"I thought you were going to look for a real job?"

I planned to take anything I could find, but I needed as much money as I could get, as quickly as possible. My plans were big, and slacking wasn't an option. "I am, but it won't hurt to have a sideline." I wiggled the ladder's feet into the soil and climbed up. "How much should I trim?"

"About two feet. It's far too overgrown, and I'd like it level with the top of the fence."

I set to work lopping the branches, and it wasn't long before I had a great view over into next door. "Did you know the neighbours have a pool?" I asked.

"Waste of money and space, if you ask me. Why anyone would spend money on something that only gets used a couple of times a year, when they could have a nice lawn instead, is beyond me."

His grumblings about people's general lack of appreciation of a good garden washed over me. My attention was occupied elsewhere. On the tiniest section of overgrown grass, behind the swimming pool, a figure was contorted into a strange position. I stared in admiration as it slowly formed another shape. Damn, she was flexible. I wondered if she was seeing anyone. If so, I hoped he appreciated what a gem he had. A woman as fine as her would know how to please a man. I could be that man. Unlike Tina, Cora was just my type—if you took away the fact that she was old enough to be my mother. Fair in colour and feminine, yet sporty, my brain began to imagine her naked, bending her body around mine, as she twisted into a new pose, met my eye, and smiled. Crap. I'd been caught peering over her garden fence like a perv. At least she couldn't read minds.

"Morning," I said, holding up the shears to prove I had a reason to be there, before severing a nearby branch.

Cora nodded, turned away, and continued with her routine, but her indifference didn't stop my eyes from drifting over, more than once, before the hedge was fully shorn.

Sunshine streamed through a gap in the curtains, making it impossible to sleep any longer. I got up and threw on my black vest top and cargo shorts. I liked to keep in shape, but gym membership was pricey, and I didn't want to waste a single penny of my savings on something I could do for free, so I planned to jog around the neighbourhood distributing my leaflets through letterboxes. The hardware store had had a no promotional literature on the counter policy, but they had allowed me to pin one onto their notice board. It was a start, but I had to get my butt in gear if I wanted to get the word out.

I managed to jog to the end of the drive before stopping in my tracks. Cora was doing stretches on her front porch.

Adjusting my bag full of leaflets higher onto my shoulder, I stared at the woman who'd been skinny dipping in her pool during my previous night's dream. And when she bent to touch her toes, I got an eyeful of creamy cleavage, bringing back memories of her pink nipples bobbing above the water. Christ, I'd love to get a handful of those beauties.

As she straightened up, she caught my eye, but pretended not to notice me.

"Nice daisies," I shouted, giving her no option but to acknowledge my presence. She narrowed her eyes and looked me up and down. Her scrutiny was intimidating, yet strangely seductive. "H-hi. How ya doing? I-I'm Johnny. I-I live next door." Stop stuttering, man. You sound like an idiot.

"Do you make a habit of staring at your neighbours?"

No. Just you. "Only when I'm wondering why they have a meadow where their lawn should be."

She had a deep, sexy laugh. I liked it. Most girls giggled and drove me nuts. Cora's laugh coated her throat like a mature wine. "It is a bit long, isn't it? But I admit I'm not friendly with the lawnmower." She strolled down the driveway, furrowing her brow as she surveyed the grass. "My husband used to take care of such things." She sighed.

"Used to?"

"He's gone."

I knew that. "I'm sorry." *No you're not.*

Her laugh surfaced again, and a hot rush swept through me. "Don't be. He's not dead. Just dead to me." Her words were said with so much venom, I wanted to ask why, but I held back. "I have been meaning to hire someone to take care of this, but it hasn't been one of my priorities."

"I could do it ... if you like."

29

She looked up through her lashes. They were the longest I'd ever seen and framed her grey eyes perfectly. "You want to mow my lawns?"

Blood hammered through my heart and I felt it all the way to my toes. How could it be possible this woman was having such an effect on me? "Mow your lawns, pull your weeds, show your garden some love. It doesn't seem to have had much lately." Fuck. Did I seriously just say that?

Thankfully my clanger went unnoticed. "It didn't have much when John was here, either. He wasn't the gardening type."

John? Shit. What a fantastic start. Now she'd be thinking about her husband every time she said my name, and most likely resent me for it. "Oh? What type was he?"

"Ambitious. When he wasn't at the office he was thinking about it. Our whole life revolved around his work." She bent her legs behind her, alternately grabbing her feet to continue stretching. "Until he left, I never realised how draining it was."

Could her legs bend forwards as easily as they bent backwards? I imagined how her ankles crushing the sides of my neck would feel. "What happened?" I asked, immediately regretting the question. I'd just met the woman and already I was prying into her life, but for some reason, I had to know.

She paused, as if unsure as to whether she should answer, before two words escaped on a breath. "Another woman."

Looking at the woman before me, beautiful, fit body, and clearly sharp minded, I couldn't comprehend any man passing her over for someone else. He must have been insane. "His loss."

She studied me, deep in concentration, and I was immediately transported back to high school, when a bunch of us were pulled into the headmaster's office after the remains of a joint was found behind B block. I'd practised my poker face that day, and was the only one not to receive detention. I used it again under Cora's gaze. If I wanted this gig, I couldn't let it show how much I wanted to get her in the sack.

"What did you say your name was?" she said.

"Johnny." I cringed as the word came out.

"Well, Johnny, I really must get on with my run, but if you're serious about helping out, come over this evening and we'll discuss the details." The end of her sentence was carried on the wind as she pressed a button on her stopwatch and set off at a pace.

Score.

Chapter Four

Not wanting to appear too eager, I killed time by taking a shower and a shave, certain that sweaty pits and stubble would not be on Cora's list of turn-ons. At the back of my drawer, I managed to find a T-shirt without a rock band logo on it, and I slapped on a helping of aftershave, for good measure.

It was eight o'clock when I knocked on Cora's door. A young girl answered. "Hi," she said. "Are you Ron's son?"

I realised she must be one of the famous daughters. "Grandson."

"That's right. Mum's expecting you. She's in the lounge. I'm Nessie, by the way."

"Johnny," I replied.

I followed Nessie into the hallway. From the back she looked a lot like her mother, apart from her clothes, but somehow, I couldn't see Cora wearing the strappy, crop top and tiny, denim hot pants, exposing the hint of ass now wiggling in front of me. I've always been an ass man, and the sight of her cute curves would normally have had me adjusting my dick, but I was strangely comfortable.

Cora glanced up from her book as I entered the room. "I wasn't sure you'd come," she said with a weak smile.

Figuring it wasn't the kind of room where tatty trainers would be welcome, I kicked off my shoes and left them at the door. "Why wouldn't I?" I asked, scanning the room in two minds about where I should sit.

Cora was curled into one end of the cream sofa, and I didn't want to encroach upon her personal space, so I stepped towards a nearby chair. She patted the cushion beside her with her French manicured fingernails. "You may have just been being polite."

I sat down next to her, leaned back leisurely, and crossed my ankles, quickly changing my mind and adjusting to a more upright position with my hands clasped between my knees. "No. I was serious. I've recently completed a degree in horticulture, and I'm looking for work," I said, trying to sound professional.

"Oh, I see. My eldest, Amy, is at university now, and my youngest, Vanessa, whom you've just met, is due to start there in September. Did you enjoy it?" Her grey eyes seemed genuinely interested.

"It was a means to an end." I didn't want to talk about uni. I hated the way it accentuated the difference in our ages and made me feel like one of her kids. "I aim to own my own business, one day."

"Gardening?"

Bit of a stupid question. "Yes. And for my first client, I'm offering special privileges." The wink that accompanied my sentence was involuntary, but every time I saw Cora, I felt myself falling a little deeper, and my body had decided it was time to start flirting.

"Which are?" Was it my imagination or was that glint in her eye in response to my wink?

"My undivided attention."

"Not that special if I'm your only client."

So not that stupid, after all. "I also have skills that don't involve vegetation." Jeez, I was at it again.

"And what would they be?"

Rein it in, Johnny. You'll scare her off. "Carpentry, for one. Ever fancied a pergola, a bit of decking. A nice place to do your yoga?"

"That's very thoughtful of you. I'll give it some consideration."

The following twenty minutes were spent discussing her garden, although her tight little sweater of soft, pink wool, practically shouting out and inviting my fingers to run over her alluring curves, ensured I wasn't paying as much attention to what she was saying as I should have been. I had to force myself to focus on her face instead of her breasts on more than one occasion. A drink wouldn't have gone amiss either. My mouth was a dry as a camel's backside, and my tongue kept getting stuck at the back of my throat. Thank Christ, I'd had the foresight to take a notebook, or I would never have remembered our conversation, and would have been without the handy boner cover when I got up to leave.

It was just my luck that it rained for four days straight—heavy relentless rain that pounded the windows and bounced of the pavements—and I had to postpone starting work on Cora's garden. Fucking British summers drove me nuts. Trust me to choose a weather-reliant career. I occupied my time by contacting an old uni friend who'd offered to design a website for me, and we ran through a number of ideas. Pappa was fascinated by the process, continually looking over my shoulder to read the exchange of emails. To fuel his interest in modern technology, I shared the workings of a software program I'd developed, recommending the best plants for various seasons and soil conditions.

The rain had kept Cora indoors too. I knew that because I couldn't resist keeping one eye on the window, hoping for a glimpse of her, as I worked. By contrast, Kendrick was hardly ever at home—and when he was, he was flaked out—offering me no opportunity to have our promised chat.

On the fifth day, the clouds broke, and, as Cora had requested, work began in the front garden of number twenty-one: starting with the lawn and moving on to forking out the dandelions. By mid-morning, I was parched, so when Cora emerged from the house with a glass of cold lemonade I took it gratefully and gulped it down.

Furtively stealing a glance at my employer, I noted she was dressed in a pretty halterneck number, lightly skimming the top of her knees and exposing her shapely calves. And considering how low the back was, there was no way she was wearing a bra. The thought heated my blood and sent it straight to my groin.

"You look nice," I commented. It was an innocent remark. She couldn't possibly take offence.

"Thank you. I'm meeting a friend for lunch," she said, taking my empty glass and placing it just inside the door. "Will you be all right here while I'm gone?"

"Are you going into town?"

"Yes."

"Driving?"

She jiggled a bunch of keys. "That's generally how I get there. Why?"

"I could do with a few supplies: weed killer, lawn seed, that kind of thing." And an excuse to be alone with you. "You couldn't drop me off at the store, could you? That is,

RAQUEL LYON

unless you already have what I need, but I didn't spot any in your shed."

"I'd be surprised if you found anything in there not covered in rust or mildew. I should have realised you might need to purchase a few things. Are you ready to leave now? I arranged to meet Diane at twelve."

Throwing the fork into the wheelbarrow, I grinned. "Sure thing. I'm good when you are."

She nodded. "Okay." She glanced down at the dirt covering my jeans. "I'll just get a cover for the seat."

I winced slightly, as I climbed into the car. Generally, I considered myself a fit guy, but my back hadn't had this much of a workout for quite a while, and I had a feeling I'd pulled something.

Cora noticed my discomfort, as she turned on the ignition. "You know, yoga is excellent for stretching out the muscles. You should try it sometime."

"Are you offering to show me your moves?" Because if she were, I could think of a few moves I definitely wouldn't mind seeing.

My innuendo went ignored, as she concentrated on the road. "I meant you should take a class. I had a very good instructor at the gym."

"Not really my style. I prefer one on one. Maybe you could teach me."

"Oh no. I couldn't. It wouldn't be right. What would people think? They might get the wrong idea."

37

In my side vision, I watched the line of her legs working the pedals. She had great legs. "Who's going to know?"

"My daughter, for one."

Leaning forward, I propped my elbow on the dashboard to look her square in the face. "I don't care if you don't. Do you approve of everything she does?"

"No, but she's young." She caught my eye and frowned. "And so are you."

"I'm nearly twenty-three."

We took a right-hand exit, and her head turned along with the car. "And I'm thirty-nine."

"That's nothing. Besides, you don't look a day over twenty-eight."

Her head shot back. "If I didn't know better, I'd say you were flirting with me, Johnny."

"Maybe a little."

"Well don't. It makes me uncomfortable."

"Why? Surely lots of men flirt with you."

"Some. And I've never been comfortable with it."

"I'm sorry. Friends it is then." If that was all she was willing to offer, I could work with it ... for now. It wasn't as if I'd expected her to just fall into my bed, although it would have made things a lot easier if she had. No. Breaking through her crusty exterior wasn't something that would happen automatically; it would have to be earned. A classy woman like Cora needed wooing, seducing, and besides, I really liked her, and she deserved more than just another notch on my bedpost. If I'd learned anything, in the past few years, it was that finding the right girl is a gamble, and I'd pushed my dick into too many slot machines, hoping to hit the jackpot. Cora was the million-dollar drop. It was time to up the stakes.

"Why? What's in it for you?" she asked, her tone steeped in curiosity.

"The pleasure of your company."

"You're a strange boy, Johnny."

"So people say."

We pulled up in the car park and the engine idled. Cora removed her purse from her bag and slipped me a couple of twenties.

"Will that cover it?"

"Should do. Thanks." I stepped out onto the tarmac. "Have a nice lunch," I said, waving her off with the twenties.

After buying everything I needed, I caught the bus back and spent another hour or so in the garden before calling it a day.

Back at Pappa's, Kendrick was slouched in front of his favourite comedy show. He offered me a cursory glance. "Where've you been all day?"

"Next door." I collapsed into an opposing chair.

"Huh?"

"At Cora's place."

TV forgotten, he held my eye. "What the fuck were you doing there? Christ. Did you score with one of those hot chicks?"

"Is that all you think about?"

He looked like shit. His nocturnal lifestyle clearly didn't agree with him. "There're worse things," he said.

"Sadly, no sex involved. The only thing I scored was a job. I'm sorting out the garden."

"That'd better be all you're sorting."

"Meaning?"

"Meaning, I'll be bummed if you bag one of those two babes before me. You gotta respect the protocol, and I saw them first."

"No worries. I've only met one of them, and she didn't give me a second glance. I tell you what, though, you get first dibs on the daughters if I get to bang the mother." I winked.

He laughed. "You're one sick motherfucker, you know that? It's a good job I know you're joking. So, are you up for another trip to the club? I put in a good word last night, and I reckon I could score you a game in the back room. Just make sure you pay up when you lose."

"I don't lose."

Chapter Five

I did lose. Twice. Then I won a small pot and lost the next.
I was only up about two-fifty, but it was all part of the
plan. If I were going to hustle these guys, I needed to test
the lie of the land before making my move. The next
round of cards was dealt and everyone bet in the first
round. I scanned the table. There were five of us
altogether. The tattooed guy opposite me was scratching
his hand, which meant he had at least a straight. The chain-
smoking, fat guy on my left folded, leaving the blond
dude, wearing an open-necked, yellow shirt, and
Snakehead, as I'd nicknamed him, on my right. Snakehead
had been the hardest to read all night. Only once had the
snake's eye above his ear twitched, and it had happened
immediately before he folded. It wasn't twitching now. He
had something, but what? The pot had crept up to over a
grand, a great night's work if I could pocket it. Yellow
Shirt called, then Tattooed Guy also folded, clearly not
trusting his luck. Snakehead lifted the corner of his cards to

check his hand, then raised. *Shit.* I had just enough to cover it, but I had to go all in, and if I lost the hand, I'd be all out for the night, and severely pissed. I thought about my four kings sitting on the table, and prayed they were enough. Yellow Shirt's cheek developed a tic as he had to go all in too, so I didn't have to wait long for the cards to be revealed. Being the last active player, he had to show his hand first. He grinned as he laid his full house on the table, smugly, but stood up so quickly that he knocked over his chair and almost tripped over it in disgust, when Snakehead produced four queens and faced me expectantly.

"Beginner's luck." I beamed, as I turned over the kings.

"Stiffed us, more like." Anger filled his cheeks with murderous blood. "No one has that much luck the first time."

I scooped up the pot from the middle of the table and patted it into a neat pile, grateful we weren't playing with chips. Somehow I got the feeling I wouldn't be given the chance to cash them in. Bravado was the only way out. "How about I come back tomorrow and give you the chance to win it all back? I'd stay but it looks like you've run out of funds."

Tattooed Guy thumped the table. "He's a fucking hustler!"

"I'm sorry. I thought that was the point," I said, standing. "Don't a bunch of you let a couple of newbies in each night and fleece them for every penny? It's my guess that this dude hasn't been in here before, either." My eyes flicked to the left and the guy shook his head, before I faced Tattoo again. "What's up, mate? Things not one-sided enough for you?"

"Watch your mouth, and get out of here before I paint it a brighter shade of red," Snakehead snarled.

"No problem. See you tomorrow," I said, with a finger flick to the temple.

❀ ❀ ❀

The next morning, I was up not long after the sun to start work on Cora's garden. There was so much shit to clear, I felt like Prince Phillip hacking his way through a wall of thorns to get to Sleeping Beauty. The wheelbarrow filled within minutes, and I wheeled it around the side of the house to deposit the cuttings in the bin.

Cora's voice drifted out from the kitchen. "I'm not interested in another relationship. My life is far too busy, and I'm too old to start again."

"Nonsense. Look at me. I'm having a great time," said another woman's voice.

I inched closer to the window to listen.

"You've never been married," Cora said. "Your great time started in your teens and kept on going."

I suppressed a snigger behind my hand. Cora had a sense of humour. Craning my head around the window frame, I looked inside. Cora's companion was perched at the breakfast bar running her hand over her excessively backcombed hair.

"Exactly. The world is too full of gorgeous men to choose just one. It's fun. You're my best friend, and without a man, you're missing out on so much of it."

"I'm perfectly happy as I am."

"No you're not." The woman laughed. "Look at you. You've got a face like a wet weekend, and if you take a break from men any longer you're going to run out of batteries. There's only one thing to put some colour back into those cheeks, and it comes packaged in a tailor-made suit. Just get this thing over with, and I'll have you back out there in no time."

Cora picked up two mugs from the counter and placed one in front of her friend. "I don't think so. You might enjoy tense evenings, pretending to be interested in your date's conversation, and laughing in all the right places, but it's not my idea of fun. You know that."

"What I know is I will not allow you to end up a lonely, old prune."

"I won't, but I am set in my ways. I don't want to hide who I really am and have to make the effort to look nice all the time. I'm past that."

"Oh, that's hogwash, and you know it. You like to look good."

Cora blew on her drink and settled herself onto the stool next to her friend. "I like to keep in shape. There's a difference. I'm doing it for me, no one else."

"All I'm saying is you can't shut yourself off from the male population, altogether. It would be such a waste of your assets." The woman turned her excessively made-up face, and I shot back against the wall before she could spot me.

"My assets are fine as they are," I heard Cora add.

I had to agree, and I decided to make it my mission to see she changed her mind about dating, but if I were ever going to have the chance to get up close and personal with Cora, I had to stop acting like a peeping perv. Turning the wheelbarrow around, I headed back to work.

The women emerged from the house as I was pruning suckers from the roses. It wasn't the best time of year for pruning, but they'd been left to run wild, and I would have been lacerated to death trying to reach the rest of the flower bed if I hadn't at least tried to tame them.

Cora waved off her friend and handed me a cup of tea. "I didn't expect to see you here this early."

I took the cup and nodded my thanks. "There's a lot to do."

As she concentrated on the clump of heather I'd had to move from beneath the rhododendron bush to a sunnier spot by the lawn, I allowed my eyes to scan down her body. She was wearing a silk robe with God knows what underneath. A co-ordinating nightdress? A lacy little two-piece? It looked like nothing but her birthday suit when a breeze rippled the silk over the peaks of her nipples, and I felt a stirring. I had to stop thinking about her naked. Concentrate on her eyes, Johnny, her eyes. "Aren't you going for your morning run?" I asked.

"Later, maybe." Her gaze moved to the ground, as she made no effort to return to the house.

"Is everything okay? You seem a bit down."

"I have to do something this morning that I haven't been looking forward to." She shrugged one shoulder as if she didn't care, when quite clearly, she did. The movement caused her robe to dip at the neckline, and exposed a hint of cleavage to my grateful eyes. How I wished I could reach under the material and expose the full glory of those enticing breasts.

"Anything I can help you with?"

"No. No. I'll be fine," she said, as she turned and disappeared back inside the house, leaving me both puzzled and aroused.

I drained my cup and, not wanting to litter the garden with dirty crockery, cautiously entered the house. The layout was similar to Pappa's place, if you discounted the fact that on the ground floor Cora's living room and kitchen had been knocked into one. I placed my cup into the sink and walked back towards the front door, but before I reached it, a faint sound of sobbing filtered down the stairway. Was that Cora crying? Of course, it was highly possible it could be her daughter, but my gut told me it wasn't.

Chapter Six

Warily, I snuck up the stairs, keeping to the edges where there was less chance of any creaking. I was definitely turning into a fucking stalker. The sobs originated from the room I knew to be the largest, and I guessed it must belong to Cora. I tiptoed up to the door. It was slightly ajar. Through the small crack, I saw her. She was perched on the edge of the bed cradling her head in her hands, dressed only in a red satin set that did nothing to dampen the semi I still sported.

I knocked lightly.

"Cora? Can I help?"

She didn't reply.

I pushed the door gently. "Cora?"

She sniffed and wiped away her tears on the back of her hand. "What are you doing up here, Johnny?"

"I went to put my cup in the kitchen and heard crying. What's up?"

"It's not your concern." She snatched at the dress lying at her side and pulled it over her head without thinking, ending up in a tangled up mess, with half of the dress snagged on the back of her head and arms everywhere. I stepped over and attempted to unhook her from the twisted cloth. "Here, let me at least help you with this."

She stood and recoiled from my touch. "I'm fine," she said, tangling herself further.

"No you're not. Stop being so fucking pig-headed and stand still."

She sighed and allowed me to remove the dress. I shook it out and lifted it back over her head. With my assistance, it fell into place with ease.

I zipped it together at the rear and stood back to admire the view. "There, that's better," I said. The red material emphasized her slight tan and highlighted her eyes. She looked so beautiful I wanted to rip the dress straight back off, lick the tears from her face, and carry on licking until there was no part of her left untasted.

"Thank you. You can leave now."

"Not until you tell me what's upsetting you."

She grabbed a tissue and dabbed her face, then picked up a hairbrush to run it through her blonde waves. "You're persistent, aren't you?"

"Yep." When I made my mind up about something, it pretty much stuck in my brain and refused to leave. My stubbornness wasn't as bad as Kendrick's, but sometimes it

—

49

was a necessity, and, this time, I hoped mine would get me into a whole other kind of trouble than his usually did.

"Why are you so interested?"

"I thought we were friends. Friends confide in each other."

The hairbrush landed on the glass top of the dressing table with a clatter, as she turned to face me. "Okay, friend. What if I said I was due at the solicitor's in an hour to sign the final divorce papers?" Her bottom lip quivered. It was full and inviting, and I wondered what it would be like to suck on it.

"I'd ask if you needed some company." She glared at me, as if not quite understanding. "Do you? Because I'd be happy to go with you." I stepped closer.

"I can't think of anything more inappropriate," she said. Her lip quivered again, and I wanted to sweep her into my arms and tell her everything was going to work out. Tell her, her two-timing bastard of a husband had never deserved her. But I resisted and settled for running the back of my fingers lightly down her arm. Her skin was as delicate as a butterfly's wing. Just brushing it made my blood pump. Fuck. I wanted more. But I wanted her to want it too, and to get that, I needed to get a mental grip on my dick. "It's personal," she said.

"Well. You know where to find me, if you feel like talking when you get back." I smiled, backing out of the door to give her the alone time she'd asked for.

———

A little more than an hour later, the side bed was neatly cleared, and I was satisfied I'd done a decent morning's work. Cora had left the door unlocked, to enable me to help myself to a drink, and I didn't want to leave the house unattended in her absence, so I wandered inside to take a look around. Everywhere was decorated in muted shades of cream and beige, with small splashes of colour added by way of soft furnishings. Expensive looking ornaments were specifically placed for dramatic effect, and modern art adorned the walls. It was a classy joint and must have cost a packet to fit out. I glanced down at my dirt covered jeans and the soil under my fingernails. Butt stains and fingerprints would not be well received. I needed a shower, badly. Stealing a glance at my watch, I wondered if I had time to grab a quick one before Cora got back, and decided to risk it.

Fifteen minutes later, I was standing in her kitchen, wearing only my boxers and drinking a glass of milk, when she returned.

I heard her before I saw her. Her small gasp of surprise caused me to turn in time to see her eyes graze over my body, and a small ripple of satisfaction pulsed in my chest. Yeah, that's right, baby. Just say the word and it's all yours.

"Um, what are you doing?" she asked, pointedly averting her gaze.

I held the glass aloft. "Drinking milk. You said I could help myself. Want some?"

"Maybe what I should have said was what are you doing in my house, naked?"

"I'm not naked. I'm wearing boxers." I pinged at the waistband to stress the fact. "And I know you noticed that."

"It's hard not to."

"I don't mind you checking me out."

Her heels clicked along the tiled floor as she slipped a leather strap from her shoulder and laid her handbag on the table. "You haven't answered my question."

"What was it again?"

"Where are your clothes?"

"On the back doorstep."

She stared down at her handbag and fiddled with the clasp. "I'd rather they were on your body."

I moved closer hoping she'd look at me again. A moment ago, I thought I'd seen a spark of interest, and I needed to kindle it. "Are you sure? They were covered with soil. I was considering your décor."

"How kind. Clearly my décor comes before dignity."

Her bag was getting more attention than I was, and I could tell she wasn't buying my excuse. Perhaps the shower hadn't been such a good idea after all. Her refusal to meet my eye spoke volumes, and I didn't want to push my luck. I had to play it cool. Change of tact, Johnny. "How did it go with the paperwork?"

Her tone softened. "I signed."

"Was your husband there?"

"No."

"Did you want him to be?"

Creases formed over the bridge of her nose. "No."

It wasn't diplomatic, but I had to know. "No love lost between you two then?"

"I hate him with the fire of a thousand volcanoes," she said, surprisingly calmly.

At any other time, I would have laughed, and I did almost choke on my last mouthful of milk, before swallowing it just in time. She had spunk, and I liked it, but this was a time that called for sensitivity. "So you don't still love him?"

"I stopped loving him a long time ago, the first time he cheated on me with my friend."

"Your friend? Not the one who was here earlier?"

"Of course not. An ex-friend."

"Understandable. So, why were you crying?"

She turned to lean on the edge of the table, steadied herself, and exhaled. "I … Well if you must know, I'm scared."

"Of what?"

"The future. One minute I had a husband and a family, and the next minute I didn't. My girls are almost grown up. They'll both be gone shortly too, and then I'll be alone. I've always been a wife and a mother. I don't know what else to do with my life."

I set my glass on the drainer and stood before her. She looked up at me with those big, grey eyes, like a frightened kitten. I took her hand and stroked my thumb across her knuckles. "You can do anything you want. You're talking as if your life is over. You're thirty-nine not eighty-nine. Look on this as a new beginning. You're a free woman now, and the first thing you have to do is decide how to celebrate."

She studied my hand but didn't pull hers away. "I'm not in a celebrating mood."

Every fibre of my being wanted to protect her, comfort her, and make her smile again. Just holding her hand was like walking into a Ferrari showroom and running your finger along the paintwork, just to see what it felt like to touch perfection, and damn, I wanted to take her for a test drive. "I tell you what, how about I make lunch for you?" I said, reluctantly letting her go and turning away.

"You can cook?" Her doubt was evident.

"Sure. I do a mean ham sandwich, or cheese on toast." I opened the refrigerator and glanced inside. As I'd expected, it was full of healthy crap. "Or salad seems to be popular here. How about some of that?"

"I usually have cream cheese and tomatoes on rye crackers, for lunch."

Ugh! I hated crackers; they tasted like cardboard. But if she liked them, I would force myself to like them too. "Perfect." I grabbed two tomatoes from the salad box, along with the tub of cheese and began opening cupboards searching for the crackers. Cora beat me to it, and we both turned to face each other at the same time. Her hands prevented full on body contact, connecting with my chest, and I automatically reached up to grasp her waist. Our eyes locked for a second, before hers fell to my lips and mine mirrored them. It was the sign I'd been waiting for. The look that told me she was interested even if she'd yet to admit it.

♠ ♠ ♠

Chapter Seven

She coughed. "Sorry. I … um …"

"Don't be." I smiled, loving the feel of her fingers on my skin so much I couldn't bear to let her go.

She pushed me away and removed the crackers from their packet, laying them on a board. I didn't miss the rise and fall of her chest under her heavy breathing, as she retrieved a knife from the drawer. "You … You're flirting with me again," she stammered.

"I get the vibe you secretly like it."

She swung to face me, knife aloft. The tip would have grazed my chin if my reflexes hadn't kicked in. "Johnny. I've just ended a relationship of twenty years. My husband was the only man in my life, and I'm not ready to be hurt by another one." Her anger surfaced, but as I tried to decide whether the cause of it was me or her ex-husband, it was the crackers that suffered, with more of them crushed under the force of the knife than ones that stayed

———

56

whole. "And when I say man, I don't mean boy," she added.

"Is that what you see when you look at me? A Boy?"

Her eyes flickered over my chest and back to the food. "No."

"I'd never hurt you," I said, swallowing a mouthful of cheesy cardboard.

Cora nibbled on a tomato. "What is it you want from me, Johnny?"

A good question. I glanced down at her curves hiding under tightly stretched material and started making a mental list. I had no idea why my need for her was so strong. Insta-lust was not a new concept to me, but this time it was fuelled by Cora's vulnerable yet self-assured spirit that could only be gained through experiencing life. Sure, I wanted to fuck her brains out, but I knew that wouldn't be enough for me. She was more than just a roll in the sack. I needed her in my life. When I looked back to her eyes, there was hint of sadness behind them which made it hard for me to breathe, let alone tell her how I felt. Underneath her crispy exterior, she was hurting. I wanted to heal her, prove that not all men are bastards, but how could I put those feelings into words without coming across as a complete prat?

She swallowed. "Just tidy up my garden, as we agreed, and try not to complicate things."

"It's only complicated if you make it so. I'm single. You're single. You really should start dating again, and I'm happy to let you practise on me." I licked spread from my finger as I waited for her to say something. She didn't. She leaned back against the counter and stared into space as she ate. "Look, I'm guessing you haven't had much fun in your life, have you? So, I have an idea. Get the rest of those crackers down you and change out of that dress into something more casual. I'm taking you out."

Her head shook. "No. You're not."

"Yes. I am. I'll be back in ten."

As promised, I returned ten minutes later, freshly clothed in a navy T-shirt and cargo shorts. Cora was cleaning the counter top, dressed exactly as she was when I'd left.

"I thought I asked you to change."

"Demanded, you mean. And I told you I'm not going anywhere. I have things to do, this afternoon."

Damn, she frustrated the hell out of me. Any other woman and I'd have called off the chase by now, and yet all I could think about was devouring her, every infuriating inch of her. "Such as?"

"Clean this mess up. Prepare tea for Vanessa—"

"Boring." I spun out the word.

"And I have brownies to make for my wine club tonight."

Bingo. Our first day out could wait. "I love brownies. Teach me how to make them." It wasn't a lie. My sweet tooth threw a bunch of cash the bakery's way with alarming regularity, but I'd never actually attempted anything homemade.

"I'm sure you have better things to do."

"Well I was going to take a beautiful woman out on a date but she cancelled at the last minute."

She pursed her lips with vexation. "I meant something that doesn't include me."

"Nope. I want to make brownies," I said resolutely.

"I'm not getting rid of you, am I?"

"I'm going to be that annoying piece of gum that gets stuck to your shoe and you can't shift however hard you try."

Her face creased into a smile, her breath blowing soft puffs down her nose. I loved that I'd made her chuckle. "Fine," she said.

When the ingredients were laid regimentally on the worktop, Cora set to work measuring them out.

"Right. What do we do first?" I asked.

"It's quite simple," she said. "Break the chocolate into that bowl, and I'll whip the eggs."

"Do I get to nibble a bit?" I asked, holding the bar to my open mouth.

She smacked my hand away, playfully. "If you're going to mess about, this is going to take all afternoon."

I lowered my eyes, sheepishly. "Sorry. Blame my grandmother."

"What for?"

"My love of chocolate. She often slipped a bar in my trouser pocket when Mum wasn't looking."

Cora's eyes flicked to my face. "Do you miss your mother?" she asked, silently instructing me to add butter to the bowl.

"Every day. But no, I'm not looking to replace her, if that was your Freudian thought."

"I didn't mean to imply …"

"It's okay. Yes, I miss my mum. I miss both my parents. Pappa is great, but he shouldn't be burdened with dependants at his age. That's why I'm aiming to set myself up as soon as possible."

The ingredients came together, and when Cora turned away, I purposely covered my hands with flour. Then when she wasn't expecting it, I grabbed her by the hips, moving her to the side so that I could stir the mixture. Her waist was slim and delicate, her hips full and firm. A small thrill warmed through me as I stole sideways glances at my handprints on her ass, as I worked. Soon I would turn them into a lasting impression.

"It's good to have ambition," she said. "By the time I was your age, I was married with two children."

"But you were happy."

"Yes. I was." She peered into the bowl. "Okay. It's ready for the tin now," she said. "I'll do it. You'll probably spill it all over the counter."

My interference had turned a routine job into a children's baking session. Cora's pristine kitchen had more than a few new pieces of artwork splattered around it, and I guessed it had taken far longer than normal to do the job, but I was pleased she didn't seem to mind. I certainly didn't. The more time I spent in her company, the more it was all I wanted to do. "Fair enough, but I get to lick the spoon."

She laughed. "My daughters used to fight over who got to do that."

"I haven't seen them around much. Where are they?"

"Amy spends most of her time at her boyfriend's apartment, nowadays. It's really only Vanessa and me now, but she's out more often than she's in. Although, I am expecting her home soon," she said, placing the tin in the oven. "It might be a good idea if you weren't here when that happens."

"Why? Are you not allowed friends?" I ran my tongue over the spoon and wiped my finger around the edge of the bowl, collecting a splodge of mixture, before spontaneously deciding to dot a blob onto the tip of Cora's nose. My question was left unanswered, when at that very moment, Nessie arrived home.

"Um, what's going on, Mum?" She stood in the doorway, surveying the scene.

"Oh, Vanessa," Cora began, as she wiped the mixture from her nose with a tea towel. "It's not what it looks like."

"Actually, it's exactly what it looks like," I said. "Two people making brownies."

Nessie narrowed her eyes. "I was told you were the gardener, not the cook."

"I'm anything your mother wants me to be."

"How nice. Did she want handprints on her bum?"

"What?" Cora twisted to see behind her, and laughed. She had dimples when she laughed, cute little dents which plumped out the fullness of her cheeks. "That was very naughty of you, Johnny."

Not half as naughty as some of the things I wanted to do to her. I shrugged. "But funny, right?"

She smiled. "A little."

I smoothed the back of my fingers down her arm. "I'd better go."

"Yes. You had," Nessie spat. "And don't bother coming back."

"Vanessa!" Cora scolded.

"It's okay," I said, holding up my hands in defeat. Nessie didn't have to like me. "I'll see you tomorrow, Cora."

♠ ♠ ♠

Chapter Eight

"You were gone all day again, Bro," Kendrick said, upon my return. He was busy clicking the console of his computer game and didn't look up as I entered.

"I have a job to do."

"Paps made a casserole. It's in the oven, if you want some."

"Great. I'm starving," I said, as I went to search out the food. Smelling chocolate all afternoon, without getting to eat the final product, had my stomach growling to be filled.

Kendrick's voice drifted down the corridor. "So, when are you gonna spare some time to spend with your baby bro?"

"How about tonight?" I shouted. "If you're thinking of going to the club, that is. I said I'd go back to the game."

"Are you sure that's wise? You were lucky to make it out of there in one piece, yesterday."

"I know what I'm doing."

"Yeah, well I hope so."

Kendrick remained focused on the screen as I curled up on the sofa with my meal. Perhaps now was a good time for that chat. "How was college today?" I asked.

"Same as always. Hate the joint. Can't be bothered. What's the point when there's fuck all out there? Ah, shit. I lost a life." He threw the controller beside him with disgust.

"You still need a qualification, and I promise, if you finish your course, it'll be all good, Rick," I said, between mouthfuls. "Look on the bright side. You've only a couple of weeks left at college."

Kendrick stretched and leaned back with his arms spread out across the top of the seating. "Yeah, but I need funds now, Bro. Liam's got a big job coming up, and he says it might warrant an extra pair of hands, if I want in." He surveyed me, frowning. "Dude, you need a haircut. You're beginning to look like Smokey."

Ignoring his jibe, I asked, "What kind of job? And who's Liam?"

"A mate of mine from the club. He does up old cars and sells them on. I guess the job's something like that. He hasn't come up with the details yet."

"Are you sure it's kosher?"

"Course. Liam's sound."

I nodded, wishing I could have been around more. If Kendrick's friends had altered in line with his appearance, I'd have liked to meet this Liam for myself. "How long have you known him?"

"All year. If you'd been here, you'd probably have been closer to him than me, by now."

"How come?"

"He's a gambler, like you."

"Poker?"

"Street racing."

Great, a tosser with a turbo. "That's illegal."

"So is unlicensed poker."

He had a point. "But poker isn't life-threatening." I shovelled the last of the casserole down my throat and set the plate down.

Kendrick sniggered. "Depends on the players." He jumped up. "You ready?"

Three thunderous faces greeted me, when I entered the poker room, making me seriously question my mentality about returning. I was no wimp, and could hold my own in a fight, but I wasn't stupid, and I didn't fancy my chances if ganged up on by the men who watched me warily as I took my seat. Still, the desire to pocket more dough was stronger than my concern over how I was going to escape the club with my face intact. Contrary to my earlier words, I'd only packed a couple of hundred into my wallet, with no intention of letting the other players relieve me of my previous night's winnings, and I fully expected to repeat my good fortune.

The evening's victims followed immediately behind me, and I didn't miss the smug look that passed between Snakehead and Yellow Shirt, who had made the change to pink, tonight—the combination of the fuchsia colour with his straw-like hair was not a good look, but the muscles straining the bright material told me I'd better keep my opinions to myself. It was clear the pair expected a bumper haul from the upcoming game, and it was almost a shame I'd have to disappoint them.

When I'd returned to accept my fate, I'd left Kendrick at the bar, awaiting Liam. Nerves about his mate's business jingled in the back of my brain, but I pushed them aside when the first cards were dealt. Distractions meant failure. I had to get my head in the room.

With six players, the pots were larger, and after a shaky start, I found my stride and thrashed the living crap out of them. It didn't go down well.

"Shitface motherfucker!" The snake's eye developed an angry twitch. "You were supposed to be losing."

"Oh yeah? Who said?"

"You did. You said we'd win it all back."

"Nah. Your brain's been polluted by too much ink. I said you'd get the chance." I bent over the table, holding eye contact as I scooped up the pot. "Not my fault you're all losers who can't hang on to your dough. I beat your asses fair and square."

Snakehead sprang to his feet, bracing his hands on the table. "I'm gonna pound your brains so hard you'll be shitting them out for a week." His two sidekicks rose and puffed out their chests, and even though I'd been expecting a similar conclusion to the evening, I'd been hoping for a less violent one. I had a quick decision to make: fight or flee. It wasn't a tough one. I backed against the door, twisted, and flung it open, before speeding through the bar as fast as I could. I never spotted Kendrick. If I had, I would have grabbed his collar and dragged him outside with me. Instead, the sound of stools falling and disgruntled calls of 'Hey, watch it fuckface', followed me into the street.

The trio was hot on my heels, but the men were old and slow, and with some nifty, evasive tactics, I was able to outwit them by ducking down a side street. I waited in the shadows, willing my lungs to refill. Then, when the sound of frustrated cussing faded into the night, I emerged and jogged home. I'd been lucky. I knew that. Mixing with the seedier section of society was a dangerous game, but a couple of grand was a couple of grand. Easy money if you lived. Shame I'd probably just used up my last chance of fishing in that ample pool.

The following day, I had a phone call. One of my leaflets had pulled through and incited a response. Two hours of pounding the pavements had, at least, turned out to be worth more than a couple of aching muscles. I was invited to meet up with the owner of a local restaurant to discuss the redesign of his outside terrace. It was precisely the kind of job I'd hoped to secure. Hardcore was an easier deal than landscaping, and promised a bigger pay cheque at the end. I was already planning it in my head, without even seeing the setup, when I started work on number twenty-one.

It was looking good. Three days of hard work had left the front of the house with a more respectable exterior, and I was pleased with my effort. All that remained were the finishing touches. I'd taken my planner along and was busy making a list of the plants needed to fill in the spaces left by the removal of dead ones, and a few annuals to add splashes of colour, when Cora emerged for her morning run.

"Hi there." I waved.

"Morning, Jonathan," she said, as she began to stretch.

Great. Just when I thought I'd cracked that hard shell of hers, she was playing it cool. "The name's Johnny. Plain old Johnny. Not short for anything, so you don't get to pull the polite aloofness with me."

She heard me but made no comment. "It's looking much better," she said, her eyes pointedly avoiding mine as they roamed from the driveway edge to the crab apple tree near the living room window. "You've done a wonderful job. I'm very grateful."

Yeah, so grateful you can't even look me at me. "It's not finished yet, and you'll be pleased to know, it's time for the best bit. We're going to make this garden as pretty as you. Are you free this afternoon? I'd like us to go plant shopping."

"You don't need me for that."

"Actually, I do. I need to know what you like."

"You're the expert. I'm sure I'll like whatever you choose."

You're not getting out of it that easily, woman. I'd been thinking up ways to spend time with her, and there was no way I was going to let her stub out one of my better ones. "I was taught to consult the clients and work with their choices. I wouldn't be doing my job properly if I imposed my taste on you."

"I really don't mind." She lifted her arms behind her head, drawing out her triceps.

Damn. This was as hard as pulling a stubborn root from the ground. "If you're not free this afternoon, I'll wait until you are, but I insist we do it together."

Her chest fell heavily. "Fine. You win. But can we go straight after lunch and not take too long? I have a hair appointment at three."

I let out a breath of satisfaction. "Twelve-thirty it is then. You have a date."

Her head shot around with a decidedly flustered expression, as she finally met my eye. "How did you know?"

My eyebrows shot up with realisation. "I meant with me, buying plants. What did you mean? Do you have another one I should know about?" My heart hammered in my chest, threatening to explode out of my throat.

"I have a date, yes, not that you need to know about it."

"Humour me."

She paused long enough for my fists to clench with jealousy at the image forming in my head. "My friend, Diane, has decided I need to meet her latest boyfriend's work colleague. She set me up without my agreement."

"And you're going? When? Tonight?"

She shrugged. "You were the one who said I should be dating again."

With me. With me. I wanted to shout, but I swallowed the words. Stay cool, Johnny. "And I meant it. It was you who insisted you weren't ready."

"Diane is very hard to say no to," she said, as she began jogging on the spot.

And I'm not? Jealousy seared up my arms and into my chest. What if she hit it off with this random dickwad, and I'd missed my chance? As far as I was concerned Cora belonged to me now, and it killed me to think of another man putting the moves on my woman. "But ..."

She ran down the driveway and waved. "Twelve-thirty," she shouted back. I stared after her, my whole body tight with envy. Fuck.

I was still rattled when I arrived home for lunch. Pappa was in the kitchen, polishing the silverware. He had a whole bookcase full of trophies from local shows. His Largest Onion and Straightest Cucumber were his favourites, and had pride of place in the centre spot, but it was his Best Hanging Basket cup that sparkled under the cotton cloth in his hand.

"Oh, hello, son. I didn't know whether or not you'd be eating at home. Sorry I haven't started to make anything yet."

"I don't expect you to wait on me all the time, Paps. I can look after myself," I said, kicking myself for my tone. It wasn't Pappa's fault I was losing grip on the one woman I'd ever truly desired. "Will soup be all right for you?"

"Soup's good." He nodded,

I pulled a can from the cupboard. "Kendrick around?" I asked, as I opened it and poured the thick liquid into a microwavable container.

"Haven't seen him all day. I've been meaning to ask you if you've had chance to have a word yet?"

"A bit, but I get the impression he wants to work rather than study. I'm hoping his absence is a sign he's actually turned up to class today." The microwave pinged and I shared the soup into bowls.

"Yes. Let us hope so. Jobs are hard to find, and doing well at college would stop him hanging around with those low lives."

"What low lives?" I asked, moving the can of silver polish to one side and replacing it with a bowl.

Pappa slurped his soup. "I've seen that Murphy boy dropping him off on a few occasions, different car every time, most likely stolen. Boys like him are bad news. Come from bad stock." He waved his spoon and a splodge of soup landed on Best Hanging Basket. He'd be pissed when he noticed that, and had to clean it again. "His father in and out of prison for pushing drugs, mother in the psych ward. What chance has a kid got with parents like that? Liam Murphy probably has his spot behind bars already reserved, and I wouldn't like to see Kendrick going down with him."

Me neither. With my worst suspicions confirmed, the urge to find Kendrick gnawed at my insides, as I wiped a piece of bread across the last of my soup, but I didn't have the time. I had fifteen minutes before I was due to meet Cora, and I still had to change.

Choosing to cover my T-shirt with a lightweight, cotton sweater—which erred on the tight side since hitting the uni gym—almost identical in colour to my thin, black jeans, I studied my reflection. Kendrick was right. A trip to the barber's wouldn't go amiss. I hadn't had a fringe that touched my nose since I was fourteen, when I first saw Sweeney Todd and refused to have my hair cut for a year. Other than that, I looked good, and I was reasonably convinced that I portrayed the right amount of maturity needed to convince Cora I could be in her life. I arrived next door at twelve-thirty on the dot.

She was waiting.

♠ ♠ ♠

Chapter Nine

I stepped inside. "Ready to go?"

She nodded and swivelled to grab her purse from the hall table. As she turned, her flirty skirt flew up to reveal the back of her knees, and the sheer, almost see-through, sleeveless blouse rippled with the movement of the air. It was a very distracting outfit. How was I supposed to keep the trip professional when she looked like that? If she wore something similar for her date, I knew exactly how much the guy would be dying to get his filthy hands on her, and the thought filled me with dread.

"You might want to put on a jacket," I noted. "It looks like rain."

"Maybe. But it's warm. I'll be fine." She paused with her key in the lock, waiting for me to exit. "Are we doing this or not?"

It was a short journey to the local DIY store, housing a small gardening section at the back, and before long, we

74

were standing amongst the plant pot filled benches, reading the accompanying information tags. I stood back and watched as Cora took pleasure in sniffing the blossoms and running her fingers through the soft tufts of the alpines. If that was her thing, I had a tuft she could finger, no problem. I noticed she was still wearing her wedding ring, and once I'd seen it, I couldn't ignore the fact. If someone had shit on me, as her husband had done to her, I wouldn't be keeping a souvenir. When she looked up and smiled, I felt compelled to ask. "Why haven't you got rid of that?" I pointed to her finger.

"What? Oh, the ring. Yes, I know I should take it off, but my finger feels bare without it. Do you think I'm wrong to leave it on?"

"You're not married anymore."

"Thank you for the reminder."

"Does the ring not do that, all by itself?"

"Not really. It's been there so long, I hardly notice it anymore." She picked up a Japonica bush. "What about this one. It will look pretty when it gets its berries."

"It will, but if you plan to have grandchildren playing in your garden anytime soon, I suggest something less poisonous, like this Astilbe."

She frowned. "The plant, I like. The reference to grandchildren, I could do without," she said.

Yeah, nice one, Johnny. Good call, you idiot.

After my gaffe, I made sure to keep the conversation strictly horticultural, and our trolley filled up in no time at all. A small amount of subtle persuasion was all it took to steer Cora's choices in the direction of what I already had in mind. Her laugh surfaced and despite her trying to distance herself from me, I could tell she enjoyed herself more than she let on. A collection of shrubs for the border and four trays of multicoloured annuals were nestled on the metal mesh, when the clouds opened, and we rushed inside under a deluge.

I shook the rain from my head like a wet dog, and my eyes were drawn to Cora's chest. Her rain soaked blouse was clinging to her hardened nipples. I couldn't help staring, and my dick twitched with interest.

Cora's eyes dropped. She bit her lip and pulled at the front of her blouse to unstick it from her breasts, but when she let go, it welded straight back.

A sales boy appeared from behind a stand, and stopped dead. He sniggered.

"What you looking at?" I snarled. "Haven't you got a job to do?"

He shrugged and returned to studying his clipboard.

Cora folded her arms over her embarrassment.

"Hate to say I told you so," I said, removing my jumper. "Here." I draped the soggy wool around her shoulders and arranged the dangling arms for optimum coverage, sneakily curling my knuckles under the cuffs to cop a small feel.

She held my gaze and shivered. "Thank you."

After a tense drive home, Cora rushed inside to change. The rain had passed and blue sky was visible between the clouds. I set about unloading our purchases from the car, and was placing the last pot on the path, when Cora re-emerged. Without meeting my eye, she handed back my jumper as I slammed down the rear door. Something was wrong. "Cora?"

"I'm going to be late," she said, as she climbed into the car, stuck the gears in reverse, and backed down the driveway. She glanced across at me before hitting the accelerator.

I had no idea what had happened. Cora had been acting perfectly normally, friendly even, up until the rain incident. After that, she'd handed her credit card over to the cashier in silence, and even though I tried to break it, the silence had continued throughout the journey back to Parkside Avenue.

Her behaviour change had happened after I touched her. Why? It wasn't the first time. She'd said nothing when I'd brushed a side boob whilst helping her on with her dress, or later that day, when I'd held her hand. And she'd laughed at the handprints on her bum. Surely, if she objected to me touching her, I'd have had a slap by now. Women were so fucking complicated.

When Cora returned from town, she brought the rain back with her. Her previously sodden rats' tails had been transformed into a smart and sexy updo of soft curls. She ran straight past me, holding her handbag over her head.

I finished planting the line of petunias, threw the potting trays in the rubbish, and entered through the kitchen door.

"Cora," I shouted. "I'm done." Receiving no answer, I walked down the corridor, heading for the stairs. "I said I'm d—" Cora stepped from the bottom of the stairs at the same time as I turned to go up them, and we almost collided.

"Oh, J-Johnny. Yes. I-I got some cash out for you. Here you are." She drew a wad of notes from her wallet. "For a job well done," she said with a weak smile.

"No problem," I said, accepting the money. "Can't wait to start on the back."

"No rush. Now I'm no longer embarrassed by frontal appearances, there's no hurry to fix the back." She walked past me with her eyes glued to the floor.

There was nothing embarrassing about her frontal appearance. I'd seen that first-hand, this afternoon. "So, you won't mind if I take a break to do another small job first, then? I'm meeting with a prospective client tonight. I mean, I might not get the gig, but ..."

The front door opened, and Cora's knuckles whitened as they gripped the knob waiting for me to exit. "Don't worry about it. Goodbye, Johnny." It was a clear brush-off, as hurtful as a stab in the gut.

"Okay. Well ..." I patted the cash against my palm with irritation. "I hope you have an enjoyable evening." Secretly, I was pissed off at her cold behaviour and hoped she had a really shitty evening, and I was kicking myself for not pressing our earlier date. Too late now. Whatever was going to happen was out of my control.

Chapter Ten

The bathwater was freezing. The heat had disappeared along with my composure. I'd tried to relax and soak away my frustrations about Cora, but the more I thought about her, the more wound up I became. Had I done something to upset her, or was her behaviour merely nerves about her date? It shouldn't bother me either way, but it did … a lot. And as much as I tried not to think about the way she'd thrown me out of her house, and would soon be making eyes at another man, a mental picture of her getting hot and sweaty with some son of a bitch pawing at her ass had buried its claws into my brain and wouldn't let go.

My meeting was scheduled for seven-thirty, and I arrived at the restaurant a few minutes early. A delicious aroma saturated my senses as soon as I entered. Decorated entirely in purple and silver, it was a high-class joint; one I could only dream about dining in. The cost of a meal alone would probably be enough to wipe out the average person's weekly wage. I glanced down at the shirt and tie I'd worn to impress, and still felt underdressed. Tailored suits and cocktail dresses filled the moulded chairs. Lights dangled over every table from metal chains, and the bar shelves groaned under the weight of the top class liquor.

I was greeted by a tuxedo-clad man and ushered upstairs to the manager's office, as if he were ashamed of my presence. Once there, I listened intently to the manager's wishes, and showed off my portfolio, before he accompanied me down to the patio area, where the work was to take place. It was not as big a job as I'd hoped, replacing a couple of dead trees, and increasing the number of planters filled with hardy evergreens. I guessed the need for speed was why I'd been chosen; my new business would be less likely to have a waiting list. The fact that it was a rush job was no problem for me. With so little to do, I'd have it completed within a couple of days. Still, work was work. A price was agreed and hands were shaken. Then I was escorted to the bar and offered a drink on the house, before I left. I accepted gratefully, having nothing better to do, and sat at the bar nursing a cold beer.

I'd almost finished my drink when a couple caught my eye. I was too far away to hear their conversation, but the man's face was stern, almost disapproving. He shook his head as he laid a hand on the woman's arm. Her distaste at his touch was obvious. She shook his hand away and stood abruptly, snatching her napkin from her lap and slamming it onto the table. Other diners halted mid-mouthful to watch the altercation. The woman turned and my heart stopped. It was Cora.

She stepped away from the table as her date stood and snagged her arm in an attempt to pull her back. Anger tore at my insides. I wanted to pummel his face into the plush furnishings. How dare he put his hands on her? I shot from my stool and was at her side in seconds. "Take your hands off the lady."

Cora's date scowled. "Mind your own business."

"It is my business. Cora is a friend of mine. So, I repeat, remove your hand from her arm."

"Or what?"

I glanced around at the faces frowning at the disturbance. This wasn't the kind of joint you started a fight in. "Or we could continue this conversation outside." Audacity puffed out my chest, as he carried out a top to toe assessment before his grip loosened and fell. "Thought not," I said.

"Johnny, were you following me?" Cora asked.

"Of course not. The meeting I told you about was with the manager of this place. I had no idea it was the same restaurant you were coming to with your date. It seems fate wanted me here."

Our dispute brought a waiter to my side. He addressed Cora. "Is there a problem here, madam?"

"No," she replied. "No problem. I was just leaving. Johnny, could you ... take me home, please?"

I beamed a gloating victory at her date, before realising I had a severe lack of wheels. Ah, hell. Who cared? We could always call a taxi. "My pleasure," I said, offering Cora the crook of my arm.

"You're leaving?" The man's acne scarred face puckered further with loathing. "With this ... boy?"

"I am. Yes." Cora snatched her shawl from the back of her chair, turned on her heels, and grabbed my arm. "Because I'm certainly ... not staying here ... with you."

His voice followed us. "You're welcome to her. Two-bit drunk."

My blood boiled, and it took all my strength to hold back. If I hadn't cared about causing a scene and getting thrown off the new job before I'd even picked up a trowel, I would have punched the fat bastard in the nose without a second thought.

As I escorted Cora towards the entrance, her heel buckled, and she stumbled into my arms. She giggled.

"Are you okay?" I asked.

"I'm a little woozy. I may have had ... one glass of wine too many."

"What, just the one?"

She clenched her teeth, and her mouth stretched over them, as she pinched her thumb and forefinger together. "I had a couple to settle my nerves ... before I came." The

83

forefinger pressed against her bottom lip. "It may not ... have been the best idea."

I suppressed a laugh. She was funny when she was tipsy. Like a little girl. "You don't say. Did you drive here?"

She nodded and pointed aimlessly in half a dozen different directions. "The Audi's over there ... somewhere," she said. Man, the drink had really taken hold. She was shitfaced.

"Where? In that tree? Or perhaps you meant inside the grocery store next door?" She slumped into my arms, her weight heavy on my chest. I held her upright.

"Please, just get me to my bed," she said.

It was everything I wanted to hear, at the worst possible time. As much as the thought made my heart ache and my dick throb with anticipation, I'd never take advantage of a woman in need. "Give me your keys before you pass out."

"You're a lifesaver," she slurred.

When I finally located the car, Cora clung to me as I eased her into the front seat. I loved the way it felt to be needed by her. I hadn't been needed by anyone since Mum died last summer, and Dad had reached out in his grief, calling for the company of his sons to remind him he still had something to live for. I'd thought he was coping, that eventually he would come to accept his loss, but he went downhill rapidly when I had to return to uni for the start of the new term, and slipped into a depression which could only ever have had one conclusion. I blamed myself. I shouldn't have gone. Maybe if I'd stayed, he'd still be alive, but I'd put my studies before my father's wellbeing. Something I've regretted ever since. Cora was suffering from a different kind of grief, but she was still hurting, and this time, I would be there to see her through to the other side.

When we arrived back at Cora's house, I carried her carefully inside and set her down in the hallway.

"Will you be okay now?" I asked, dropping her purse onto the table.

"I'll be fine," she said, moving away from my supportive arms and stumbling once more.

I caught her around the waist. "Maybe I'd better see you to your room."

She looked at the stairs and blinked. I followed her thought process. She'd never make it up the stairs alone. Before she could protest, I scooped her into my arms and carried her up to the bedroom, lowering her feet gently onto the bedside rug. Her arms twisted behind her back, attempting to find the zip of her dress, and I bit back a chuckle as she contorted like Mr Elastic Man. "Here. Let me."

Without protest, she allowed me to slide down the zip and let the dress drop to her ankles, revealing a black push-up bra and matching panties, which fuelled my now pulsating hard-on. I had to dig deep into my reserve to resist the urge to assist her off with the sexy little two-piece too. Since meeting Cora, I'd been in a constant state of sexual frustration, and it took every ounce of my willpower not to strip her fully naked and fuck her 'til the sun came up, but now wasn't the time. I eased her under the covers and laid a soft kiss on her forehead. "Goodnight, beautiful."

Her lips parted and a word that was barely a whisper escaped. "Stay."

What was that? I wasn't sure I'd heard her correctly. The permanent horn taking up residence in my groin could be causing me to hear what I wanted to hear. I squatted down to level my head with hers. "Did you say something?"

Her eyes flickered open. "Stay," she repeated.

Yep, I'd definitely heard her right, and needing no further invitation, I stripped off and slipped under the sheet, fully expecting her to roll over and plant me with the slap I'd been expecting, because she hadn't actually meant for me to join her in the bed. But hey, nothing ventured, nothing gained. I lay on my side, wondering what to do next, when she surprised me by reaching around to pull my arm over her body, and wriggling into me. I inched closer until we were spooning with my bulging erection nestled exactly where I wanted it, between her ass cheeks. She smelled of heady perfume and stale wine, a pungent mixture that invaded my nostrils and made my temples throb, but the pain was nothing in comparison to the agony of being so close to something so unavailable.

I waited until I was certain she was asleep, before I snuck to the en suite and jacked one off. I knew I shouldn't have, but hell, I'm a red-blooded man, and if I hadn't done it, my load would have blown, in the middle of the night, all over her peachy little ass. When I returned, Cora rolled over and nestled into my chest. My heart was beating so loudly I thought she would wake, but instead, her breathing slowed and her body melted into mine.

I could get used to this.

♠ ♠ ♠
Chapter Eleven

When I awoke, nine hours later, Cora was in the same position, with her face sporting a crooked smile and her hand wrapped around my morning glory. I considered rousing her, to ask her to move it, but it felt so good I was already on the verge of exploding. My yawning caused her eyelids to flutter open, and recollection startled her upright, clutching the sheet to her chest. "Johnny? No. Please say … no."

My face creased to a smile. "No."

"Then … Why are you in my bed?"

"Because it's where you wanted me."

"I did?" She looked puzzled.

"Yeah." I laughed. "You did."

"Oh my God, what have I done?"

"You got a bit tipsy, that's all."

"And invited you into my bed?"

"Yeah."

Her eyes hardened. "You should have said no."

"I don't like to disappoint."

She lifted the sheet, looked down at her body, and relaxed with relief. "And then what did I do?"

"You fell asleep."

"Is that all?"

"Well, you snored a little."

"I don't snore."

"It was cute."

She bit her lip nervously, giving her an innocent air. "But my hand was on your ... You know."

I loved how I was making her uncomfortable. I'd half expected her to scream at me to get out, but she hadn't. She liked me. I knew it. "Yeah, baby. I didn't mind. In fact, I enjoyed it. You can put it back, if you like."

Her eyes closed and she let go of a sigh. "What happened last night?"

"Your date didn't go too well. I gave you a ride home."

Her eyes flickered along with her thought process. "You'd better go."

"If that's what you want." It wasn't what I wanted. I was exactly where I wanted to be ... almost. I'd stupidly thought that maybe our night together would bring us closer. Instead, she was slinging me out without so much as a thank-you. If I'd been kicked in the stomach, I couldn't have felt sicker.

She paused just long enough to offer me a glimmer of hope. "It is."

I couldn't leave without trying to hold on to the ground I'd gained. "All right. On one condition. Come out with me today."

"I can't."

"Do you have plans?"

"No."

"Then why not?"

She gripped the sheet tighter. "I can't do this."

"You were doing fine a minute ago."

"Johnny, please. I'm embarrassed enough as it is."

"What's to be embarrassed about?" I laid a hand on her Egyptian cotton covered knee. Her breath caught.

"Listen, Johnny, I like you. You've been good to me. I thank you for bringing me home, but I can't go out with you."

"I need a reason."

She stared at my hand, and her voiced wavered. "I-I just can't."

"I thought you'd started dating again."

"That wasn't my idea." Her fingers rubbed across her forehead and her eyes squeezed shut for a second.

"But you went anyway, and you owe me one for rescuing you last night."

Her mouth opened in silent protest. Closed. And opened again. "Fine. You can take me out. Once. But that's it, okay?"

A foot in the door was all I needed. I squeezed her knee playfully and climbed out of bed. "Morning or afternoon?" I asked, retrieving my pants from the floor and stepping into them.

She tried not to watch, but she did. "Um, oh, um ..." She rubbed her brow again. "If I can rid myself of this headache, I still intend to take my morning run."

"Okay," I said, pulling on my shirt. "I'll come round at two. No need to change out of the Lycra."

I turned from Cora's puzzled expression and jogged down the stairs, just as Nessie entered the front door. I winked at her, in passing.

"What the fuck ...?" she shouted, staring at my open shirt. "Mum? Mum?"

I glanced back to witness her taking the stairs at a pace, wondering how Cora was going to explain my unkempt presence, upstairs, at seven o'clock in the morning.

❀ ❀ ❀

Back at Pappa's, the air was eerily quiet, with only the faint rumble of snoring filtering through Pappa's door. No sound emitted from Kendrick's room. Most likely the result of another late night making him dead to the world.

I tried to keep the noise down as I took a welcome shower, but almost cursed out loud when I saw the empty shampoo bottle. Paps liked to have a long soak his en suite, so I knew it had to be Kendrick who had nicked the last of it, and we were out of shower gel too. Fucking typical. I'd almost forgotten what it was like to live with my brother's inconsiderate ways. With no option left, I grabbed the only thing available and washed myself with conditioner. Then with coconut wafting in the air, I changed into a fresh pair of jeans and a T-shirt retrieved from the floor—I'd only worn it for a day and it didn't smell overly ripe.

Suitably refreshed, I jogged downstairs to kick-start the coffee machine. Not that I needed coffee. My energy levels were sky high from the impromptu early night and my progress with Cora, but Paps would appreciate my effort when he rose for the day. The audible bubbling of the percolator was overtaken by a crash, as the front door burst open. I rushed to see the cause.

In the doorway, a muscular, sandy haired guy held Kendrick draped, unconscious, at his side. He struggled through the opening with his burden. "He got a bit roughed up, mate. He's all yours."

I studied my brother's bruised and bloodied face. His skin was warm, and a pulse met my fingers on his neck. "What happened?"

"Fucked if I know. I found him like this."

"Yeah, right. Where?"

"In the gutter. Back of Green Street."

"And you're saying you had nothing to do with it?"

"Would I have brought him home, if I had?"

"Who are you?"

"Name's Liam," he said, unhooking Kendrick's arm and pushing his body in my direction. His bulk slumped into me as I caught him.

Liam, of course. Who else? "If you did this to him, I'll …"

"You'll what? Christ. You do a guy a favour and get shit for gratitude. Fuck you. Try taking a look in the mirror before laying blame at someone else's door."

Struggling under the dead weight of my brother, I asked, "What's that supposed to mean?"

"Rick was doing fine before you turned up. Then you come waltzing onto our turf, acting all big man. Feathers have been ruffled, cockshit," Liam's narrowed eyes stared down his nose, "and we don't need you stirring up more trouble. When he comes round, you can tell him the job's off, and he's got you to thank."

Vibration shuddered through the house as the door slammed under the force of Liam's wrath. I stared at the woodwork, covering the opening where he'd stood a second ago, and hitched Kendrick more securely into my hold. The metallic smell of blood coated my nostrils.

Kendrick groaned.

"Come on, Bro. Better get you upstairs before Paps sees the state you're in."

If Pappa woke up and saw his grandson battered and bruised, any points I'd earned with my coffee making skills would be outshone, big time, by my failure to keep Kendrick out of harm's way.

How had it come to this? I'd been in town less than a fortnight. Before I arrived, I had very specific plans. Plans for a secure future for both Kendrick and me. Plans that hadn't included falling for Pappa's next-door neighbour or making enemies in my new town. Kendrick was my baby bro. I was meant to be taking care of him, keeping him out of trouble, but if Liam was right, all I'd done, so far, was to get Kendrick's face pulped. It had to have been those sadistic bastards from the game. If I hadn't gone back, my brother would have been safe. If they'd caught me that night, it would have been me lying in the alley, not him. Why was I so stupid as to think I'd get away with it? All the cash in the world couldn't replace the life of my brother.

For the second time in a few short hours, I carried someone upstairs, this time with my guilt weighing down my burden.

I made Kendrick as comfortable as possible, cleaning away the dried blood and propping up his head with plenty of pillows. There was nothing more I could do, short of a trip to the hospital, and that would mean questions I couldn't answer, and possibly the police. Involving the authorities would only cause more trouble. Incidents like this were always outside the law.

Blood had stained my already suspect T-shirt, which forced me to finally do some laundry. I swear if I ever make it in life, I'm hiring a laundry service to do that crap. Dealing with your own stench is bad enough, but other people's sweat stains and skid marks make me dry heave.

Paps surfaced when I was stuffing the machine.

"I made coffee, although it might be stewed by now. Should I make fresh?" I asked.

"No need to trouble yourself," Paps said, pouring a cup. "I'm sure it'll be fine."

I watched as he shuffled down the corridor, coffee in hand, pulled the morning paper from the letterbox, and settled into his chair. Moments later, the air filled with tobacco aroma.

So much for point scoring.

♠ ♠ ♠

Chapter Twelve

Newly clothed in a fresh, white T-shirt, I stood on Cora's front porch with a bicycle in each hand, contemplating which one to let go of in order to knock.

The bicycles had belonged to my parents and had been sitting in Pappa's garage, gathering rust for a year, along with boxes full of other memorabilia that Pappa couldn't bear to get rid of. It was time they had an outing.

I'd checked in on Kendrick before I left, but he was out of it, and I thought it best to let him sleep. He could tell me what happened later. Pappa had enquired as to his whereabouts, and I contemplated telling him that Kendrick had gone to college, but if he woke up, or if Pappa went into his room for some reason, I'd be in trouble. Hell, I'd be in the shit anyway. I'd said Kendrick wasn't feeling well and wanted to be left alone. Pappa had drawn his own conclusion and grumbled something about too much beer. I hoped it was enough to prevent him from poking his nose around the door and exposing my lie, but I wasn't holding my breath.

Finally plumping for the old lean the bike against the leg method, I knocked. It wasn't long before I got an answer.

As usual for our relationship, Cora had totally ignored my request. Not a patch of Lycra in sight. Her tie fronted top and tight capri pants, which left nothing to the imagination, would have to do. She looked down at the bikes, and frowned. "What are those?"

"A couple of elephants. What do they look like?"

"Is this is your idea of a date?"

"Actually, I figured it would be more your idea of a date. You know. Something sporty. And let's face it, your wine and dine thing didn't work out too well. What's up? Can't you cycle?"

"Of course, I can." She paused for a second and her brow furrowed. "Or I could ... thirty years ago."

"You haven't been on a bike since you were nine?"

She shook her head. "I outgrew my old one, and my parents couldn't afford a replacement. I haven't had cause to cycle since."

"Well, it was either these or the sledge. Although, if you fancy trying that, I might be able to rustle up a couple of Huskies ..."

Her nose wrinkled. "Scary eyes,"

"That settles it, then. Don't worry. It's like riding a bike." I laughed.

Cora wobbled, at first, but I rode alongside her, grabbing the saddle on occasion to prevent an unwanted familiarity with the road, and by the time we arrived at the park, she was much steadier.

The sultry afternoon had brought life to the rolling grasslands. Mothers congregated in groups, watching their small children run in circles; joggers paced in time with the music filling their ears, and clusters of teenagers, enjoying their first days of academic freedom, kicked around balls or slurped from cans which most likely held liquid far more potent than the outer artwork illustrated. It reminded me of my own schooldays, when illicit drinking with my mates was the highlight of any day.

I shouted over to Cora, "Need a rest?"

She nodded.

We pulled up under an old oak tree. I propped the bikes against it and reached into my backpack for a specially prepared package.

"I hope you like red," I said, as I unrolled the picnic blanket. "I gathered from the contents of your refrigerator that you're a wine fan, but I haven't the first clue about the stuff." Inside the blanket were a bottle and two tumblers. "I nicked this particular vintage from Pappa's wine rack. He didn't have white," I added, laying the bottle on the ground, in order to spread out the blanket, and beckoning Cora to sit down.

"Are you sure we should be having alcohol?" she asked, over the sound of the cork popping.

"Still hung over?"

She watched the red liquid fill the glasses. "I meant with the bikes," she said, accepting her glass and staring into it. "What if we get stopped by the police?"

I cracked a smile. "What, drunk in charge of a bicycle?"

"It happens. I've seen it on television."

"Yeah, if you're a pisshead. Seriously, you looked drunk enough, wobbling all over the road, on the way here. I doubt anyone would notice the difference."

Cora pretended to take offence, affording me a small slap to the thigh, as she sipped on her drink and sloshed the liquid around her mouth. "Mmm, this isn't bad."

Wine was wine to me. I couldn't tell good from bad and, given the choice, would have preferred a beer or whisky, so I downed mine in one gulp and laid back, letting the warmth radiate around my stomach.

The sun twinkled through the canopy of leaves over our heads. Life was good. Only one thing could make it better, and I could feel the weight of her stare. A huge grin stretched across my face.

"What are you thinking?" Cora asked.

I turned my head. "Do you believe in heaven?"

"Why do you ask?"

"Look." I pointed up to the tree.

Cora shuffled her bottom down the blanket to lie beside me. "What am I looking at?"

"I was thinking the sun looks like angels' wands twinkling."

"Angels don't have wands."

"They did in my school plays."

"Were you an angel?"

I smiled at the irony. "I've never been an angel. I was usually a sheep. I did once get promoted to a wise man, but I dropped the gold on Baby Jesus's head and it didn't go down too well." Her laugh surfaced again, and I felt her walls crumbling. "What about you?" I asked, rolling over to face her.

"What about me?"

I propped up on my elbow and studied Cora's face. Her cheeks were flushed from the exercise; her eyes reflected the twinkles. She was my angel. "Tell me about your childhood."

"I was the Virgin Mary."

No surprise there. "Teacher's pet?"

"Teacher's daughter."

"Mother or father?"

"Father. My mother has health problems. She hasn't worked for years."

"I'm sorry." Without thinking, I snapped off a long blade of grass and rolled it between my fingers. "What about siblings?"

"Just me."

"What was that like?"

"Quiet. Lonely at times. But I had a lot of friends. I was happy." I trailed the grass up her arm and she shivered.

"Are you cold?"

Her eyes flicked to mine. "No. Why do you ask?"

"No reason."

I wanted to kiss her so fucking badly. I wanted to touch her for real, not with an inanimate object but with my fingers running over her silken skin, exploring places left untouched for too long. Screw that. I didn't just want it, I needed it, and the way she was looking at me told me she wanted it just as much as I did—even if she was still refusing admit it. But I was afraid to spoil the moment. It was too perfect. Her hard edges were softening but I wasn't sure she was soft enough. The grass continued its journey across her enticing slice of bare stomach. Her lips parted and a puff of breath shot out, quickly replaced by a sharp intake. Yeah. She was soft. I leaned closer, until my nose was inches from hers. Maybe this *was* the moment.

"Don't," she said.

"Don't what?"

"Kiss me."

"Who said I was going to kiss you?"

"Weren't you?"

"I thought about it." I must have thought about it over a thousand times, since I'd first laid eyes on her. "Who wouldn't?"

"Well stop thinking about it."

"Why?"

"You know why."

A haze of moisture glistened over her perfect cupid's bow, inviting me to run my tongue over it. Lips like hers deserved to be kissed. If it were up to me, I'd keep them plumped and puckered all day every day. Starting now. What would she do if I tried, hit me, push me away? Was it worth the risk? It might be.

"Actually, I don't remember our kissing discussion. Fancy running it by me again?" I discarded the grass but continued the stroking, drawing circles around her belly button.

"I, um ..." Her mouth stayed open as her eyes closed. My touch had rendered her speechless. I saw my chance and bent my head to her collarbone. When my lips made contact, I passed the point of no return. The pounding in my chest refused to be ignored. Static charged blood through my veins and my dick sprang into action. Down boy. Patience. A moan shivered through Cora. It was all the encouragement I needed. I gripped her waist and moved up her neck to nibble on her earlobe. She smelled of vanilla and lilies; it was intoxicating, and my head whirled with her scent.

She sucked in a breath, and her hand gripped my arm, lifting it away as she pushed up to standing. "I have to get back."

Damn the woman. What was it going to take for her to let me in?

♠ ♠ ♠

Chapter Thirteen

Kendrick stirred and winced, as I entered his room, later that day. "Shit, my head's banging. What happened?"

"You tell me."

He pressed a hand over his face, feeling the swelling. "My face is fucked."

"Tends to happen when you come in contact with a fist or three. How do you feel?" I asked, opening the first-aid kit. "Dizzy? Sick?"

"Nope. Can't feel anything through this damn pain." He groaned. "Do I still have all my bits?"

"You might be missing a spot of brain, but let's face it, that's not much of a loss. Your bits, you can check for yourself." Kendrick tried to laugh but it came out as a grimace, switching to a growl, as I parted wedges of hair packed with congealed blood. "Did you see who did you over?"

"Nah, man. Got jumped from behind. Whacked me with something hard. I thought my head was going to explode." His face repeatedly crumbled and his teeth ground together as he talked. "Next thing I know, I'm on the ground, boots coming from all directions. How did you find me?" he asked, watching me remove items from the first-aid box.

"I didn't."

"Then who?"

"Liam."

He forced a grin. "Told you he was a top mate."

"You might wanna rethink that. He wasn't too friendly this morning."

"He's just wary of dudes he doesn't know."

I soaked a cloth with antiseptic and cleaned his wounds for the second time in a day. "Hostile was more the word I had in mind, and he said to say the job's off."

"Really? Crap. I was counting on that." He swatted at my hand. "Jesus, is that acid?"

"Shut up and hold still."

"Did he say why?"

"He didn't stop to chat."

"Man, I needed that money."

"Then get a proper job."

"Get serious."

With the cuts more exposed, I was thankful they appeared less severe than at first thought. He should be able to get by without stitches, if I held the skin together with sticking plasters, but it would probably leave a scar, in any case. The swellings covering his face were worse. I had to remember what he looked like to know my brother was hiding beneath them. "Why are you so desperate for cash?" I asked.

"I wanna do something."

"Such as?"

"You wouldn't like it."

"Then you'd better not do it," I said, smearing cream over the worst scrapes.

"You're not my dad."

"If I have no say, why bother with the secrecy? Unless you give a shit what I think."

"I wanna get some wheels, all right?"

"Can you even drive?" I handed him a couple of painkillers and he shot them back.

"Course."

"You have a licence?"

"Well, no. But I will. Soon. That's why I need the cash."

Kendrick wanting a car was no surprise. I'd expected it. He'd have all the money he needed when he hit twenty-one and came into his share of Mum's life insurance, but patience didn't come easy to Kendrick, and my sympathy was in short supply. "Not getting why you thought I wouldn't be okay with that. What are you not telling me?"

"The car ..."

"Yeah?"

"I wanna race it."

Hell, no. "You can fuck that idea off, right now."

"See. I fucking knew it. You're such a douche. Lighten up."

"You've no experience. At all."

"I'll get some."

"Uh-uh. No way. I am not going to another funeral."

"I'll be careful. Just do the small races, not the big stuff."

"Not on my watch." He was in no fit state for an argument, but there was no chance in hell I'd be letting him risk his life for an adrenalin kick. "This conversation isn't over, but I'm not being responsible for you popping a blood vessel." I smashed the tube of cream and packet of tablets back into the first-aid box and slammed it shut. "I'll bring food up soon."

The evening dragged. I spent the majority of it in front of the TV, watching a film with Paps and sketching out ideas for Cora's rear garden. But it was hard to concentrate under the deluge of Pappa's comments about continuity errors and how modern films had too many special effects and not enough storyline. I tried to humour him. The old man had been short of company since Gran's death, and I doubted Kendrick had been of much use in that department. When the film finished, I left Paps doing his late-night crossword, checked in on Kendrick, and got my head down.

The next morning, I started work at the restaurant, and completed it a few days later, well within the timescale I'd predicted. It would have been quicker had I not had to wait for a delivery of topsoil.

Despite my job keeping me busy, my mind constantly wandered to thoughts of Cora. I could still taste her skin on my lips, hear her sighs in my ears, and feel her body touching mine. I ached to be with her again, and wondered if she was thinking about me at all. I'd decided to try the absence makes the heart grow fonder tact, but so far, I had no clue as to whether it was working. All I knew was, a few days without so much as a sighting of her was more than I could handle, and I was beginning to panic that our time apart was undoing any progress I'd made. On the last day of the job, I caught the bus home and resolved to call round to see her, that evening.

A couple of streets from home, the bus pulled in at the stop in front of the Pocket Scratcher. Down the side alley, three men stood huddled behind the dumpsters, and an altercation was taking place. I recognised two of the men as Snakehead and Tattooed Guy. They had the third man cornered, and Snakehead was waggling something small and white in his face. An old lady shuffling along the aisle distracted me for a second, and when I turned back to the alley, Tattooed Guy was holding the third man's arms behind his back, while Snakehead pummelled fists into his stomach. I felt every punch as if it were me. It should have been me instead of Kendrick. The old lady took her seat, the bus set off, and I saw no more.

When I arrived home, I went straight to Kendrick's room. He had finally dragged his scrawny ass out of bed, and with the swellings receding, looked marginally more human. The scratches had scabbed over, and his bruises had changed from purple to an odd mixture of green and brown. He was sitting on his bed, lacing up his boots, as I entered.

"Where do you think you're going?" I asked.

"Out."

"No shit. Where?" I didn't have time to babysit him tonight.

"Don't bust a brain cell. I'll keep out of trouble." Kendrick shot to his feet and grabbed his jacket from the floor. "Lexi's at a loose end, and I need my kicks, man. I'm going nuts holed up in this room." He delved in the pocket, noted the presence of a condom, and tossed the jacket over one shoulder. "Wanna come? I can ask if Tina's free too."

"Nah, I'll pass on the walking STD this time, thanks. I've got other plans."

"What plans? You hooked up without telling me?" he asked, contorting his face as if the possibility were laughable.

I followed him out of the room and jogged down the stairs. "I'm working on it."

"Yeah? You have someone in mind? Who is it? Do I know her?"

"Kind of."

He turned to face me. "Really? Who? Is it that hot chick from the burger joint?"

"Nah, I'm after some higher class action."

Pappa's voice prevented Kendrick firing any more questions my way. "Kendrick? Is that you? Feeling better?" He wandered into the hallway. "Good grief. You don't get those from any illness I know." Pappa scowled at me. "I expected better of you, Johnny. You told me he was ill and you were taking care of him. You've been lying to me for days."

"I'm sorry, Paps, but I didn't want to worry you," I said, wondering how in hell I was going to explain why his grandson's face was six shades of messed up. I didn't have to.

Pappa grabbed Kendrick's chin, and turned his head from side to side. "Who did this?"

"No one, Paps. Bike crash," Kendrick said, wincing slightly.

"What bike?"

"My mate's. I was riding pillion. We rode out of town. A few of them were racing, and the bike I was on got out of control and crashed into a tree. I rolled down the banking into a pile of twigs and crap. Scraped the shit out of me."

"You were racing? It was that Murphy boy wasn't it? I knew he'd get you into trouble. Why weren't you wearing a helmet?"

"I was. Strap snapped. Helmet came off. It's nothing, Paps. Don't fuss."

I had to respect my brother's genius. If there had been a medal for bullshit, he'd have earned his stripes with that excuse.

Paps continued his interrogation. "Have you been to hospital?"

"No need. It was only a couple of bumps and scrapes. I'm good."

"You should still get looked over. Banging your head is dangerous."

"I said I'm good." Kendrick made a break for the exit. "See you later."

Pappa watched the door close, before his attention slid back to me. "Idiot boy. He's a danger to himself. Who gets injured in a road accident and doesn't go to hospital?"

How could I answer without more lies? "Some people, I guess."

"Hmm."

"Don't you believe his story?"

"I'm not sure I believe anything that boy says, nowadays." Pappa shuffled into the lounge, as I headed for the kitchen to grab a bite. Nerves over my visit to Cora had snuffed my appetite, but I knew I should eat something. I settled for a banana.

"There's a documentary on about plant life, in half an hour. I thought we could watch it together," Pappa called.

"Love to, Paps, but I have to go out, and I don't expect I'll be back in time."

"I didn't catch that."

"I have to go out," I shouted, louder this time, as I discarded the peel and took a bite.

"Work again?" he asked, when I stuck my head around the doorway.

"Hopefully."

"Maybe catch the repeat, then."

"Sure, no problem," I said, stuffing the last of the fruit down my throat, as I left.

♠ ♠ ♠

Chapter Fourteen

I stopped on the doorstep of number twenty-one, smoothed my unruly fringe from my eyes, and cupped my hand over my mouth to check my breath. I hoped Cora liked eau de banana. At least, I'd had a sandwich, and not my usual pizza, for lunch. Banana was preferable to stale garlic.

Taking a deep breath, I knocked.

The door opened, and Nessie glowered through the crack. "Oh, it's you. Tired of mornings, are we? Didn't want to pop in again at sunrise and assault my mother again?"

Assault her? "Excuse me?"

"She told me."

What the fuck had Cora said? "Told you what?"

"About your dawn visit. The urgent business that couldn't wait. The business that was so important you seem to have forgotten about it. What's that fucking urgent about gardening? Please enlighten me, because I haven't the first clue."

"Oh, that. Your mother didn't tell you?"

"She said I wouldn't be interested, but believe me, I am. So, come on, spill."

Kendrick's talent for lying would have been handy at that moment, unfortunately, I wasn't as gifted. "I'm sure if Cora wanted you to know she would have told you."

"Look. I don't know what's going on with you two, but something is, and I don't like it. Things have changed around here."

"What do you mean?"

"Mum's not Mum. She wanders around like she's not even here. The house is a mess, I have to make my own meals, and she isn't interrogating my every move. It's not normal." She angled her head and narrowed her eyes. "Are you fucking her?"

My eyebrows shot up at her candour, and I almost choked on my own spit. "No!" *Not yet.* "I can't believe you asked that. Look. Can I come in or not? I need to talk to her."

Nessie chewed over my request, before shouting, "Mum. You have a visitor." She left the door ajar and disappeared from view.

My grin spread wide at Cora's appearance.

"Johnny? I-I wasn't expecting you." She tucked a strand of hair behind her ear and noticeably swallowed.

RAQUEL LYON

"Nice surprise?"

"Um, have you come about the garden? I said there was no rush."

"I know. Can we talk inside? As nice as your doorstep is, it's been a long day, and I wouldn't mind sitting down."

"Yes. Yes, of course."

The door opened wider, and I followed Cora into the living room. Nessie was already curled up on the sofa: headphones over her ears, magazine in hand. Cora sat down rigidly on the opposite seating and clenched her hands together. I joined her, leaving a respectable gap between us.

"Are you all right?" I asked, flicking my eyes over to Nessie. Those headphones had better be on full volume.

Ignoring my question, she nodded at the sketchbook in my lap. "Was there something you wanted to show me?"

"Huh? Oh. Yeah. It's just some ideas I had, but they can wait. I want to talk about what happened the other day."

"Please, Johnny. Now is not the time." Her eyes held a warning.

Nessie's presence was annoying and unpredicted. I hadn't banked on her being at home, let alone in the same room. In my desire to see Cora, I hadn't thought things through. I needed to get her alone. It was time I made my move. I'd waited too long, and damn it, I had to know where I stood.

115

Nessie was positioned with her back to the kitchen area, so, banking on Cora being the perfect hostess, I said, "I wouldn't say no to a drink."

"A drink?"

"Yeah. You know. The liquid stuff that comes in a glass."

"I know what a drink is, Johnny."

"Then you won't mind getting me one. Anything will do."

Cora sighed, stood, and wandered off in the direction of the kitchen. I waited all of four seconds, and followed her. Nessie's gaze followed me.

In the kitchen, Cora was securing the top on a half-used bottle of gin.

"Fancied the hard stuff, huh?" I noted.

She pulled a bottle of tonic from the refrigerator. "It was already open, and you said anything," she said, twisting off the cap and holding the glasses as she poured. Her hand trembled so much she missed the second one and splashed liquid on her fingers. "Shit," she said, licking off the droplets.

I let out a small laugh. "That's the first time I've heard you curse," I said, stepping closer to prise her hand from her lips and pull it to mine.

Our eyes locked as I took her fingers into my mouth and ran my tongue down the creases. Her eyelids fluttered gently, and her chest rose and fell rapidly. Fuck it. It was time. I couldn't hold out any longer. Hooking my arm around her waist, I closed the space between us, released my mouth from her hand, and sealed it to her lips before she had the chance to stop me. She stiffened but didn't object, so I let go of her hand and reached up to her neck to caress her jaw, holding her to me as I pressed my tongue into the line of her lips. Christ, I had to get in there. I had her. I knew it. I could make her mine, if she would just …

Cora relaxed. Her arms reached up my back, and her lips parted. A split second was all it took for my tongue to find hers. She responded, tentatively at first, then eagerly. All my pent-up frustration spilled out, and I left no part of Cora's mouth undiscovered. She softened into me. Her pliable body squeezed tightly against mine. The touch of her fingers on my shoulder blades, and her breasts pressed against my chest, made my blood run hot and head straight to my groin, causing the hard line of my dick to push urgently into her stomach, alerting her to just how much I wanted her.

All too soon, she pulled back and gasped. "I can't breathe."

"I'm sorry. I've wanted to kiss you for so long. I got carried away."

"It's not that."

"Then what?"

"I-I want … No. I shouldn't have let you …" Her words were resisting, but her eyes begged for more.

"Let me what? This?" I lay soft kisses on her cheek, her jaw, her chin, her lips.

"Johnny, please ..."

Before she could finish her sentence, Nessie strode into the kitchen, face full of anger, and planted her hands on her hips. "I fucking knew it!"

Jeez, could I never get a break?

Cora stepped back, startled, stumbled on a chair leg, and braced herself against the kitchen table. "Vanessa. It isn't ... We weren't ..."

"Yes, you were," Nessie said. "I saw you."

I grinned. "Jealousy's a killer."

"As if. It's disgusting. Sick." Nessie threw her hands in the air. "Are you having a midlife crisis, Mum? No. Don't answer. I can't deal with this shit. It's wrong on so many levels. I'm going to Jess's."

Silence hung in the kitchen until the front door slammed shut. I stepped over to Cora and took her by the shoulders. "I guess that means we're alone."

Cora's eyes slowly met mine. "Johnny, what are we doing?"

I bent my head to her neck. "Getting it on," I said, dropping kisses on her neck. If I had to kiss her a thousand times to get her to admit defeat, I would. No way was I giving up now. Not now I'd nibbled the frosting. Now, I had to have the whole delicious cake.

"But, Vanessa ..."

"Forget her. This isn't about her; it's about you … and me." My hand moved slowly down her neck to the top button of her blouse, and popped it open.

"But …"

I continued down the line of buttons, slowly releasing each one. Black lace. Perfect. My favourite. "No. No buts, no more excuses, no more waiting." I parted the material and drank in the sight of her breasts, cupping one in each hand and running my thumbs over their supple swells. "This is gonna happen."

Her knuckles whitened as she gripped the tabletop harder and arched her back to me. "Why me?" She gasped. "Why me, when there're thousands of girls out there: younger, prettier girls? Oh God, that feels good."

"I don't want them. I want you. You're a smart, sexy woman, and I think about you every moment of every day." I teased down the lace and bent my head, eager to see her pert nipple and taste its sweetness.

She didn't let me get that far. "Stop, Johnny. Please stop."

Was she serious? "Why?"

She pushed her hands up between us and pulled the front of her blouse together. "Just stop."

Chapter Fifteen

I collected the drinks and followed Cora to the living room, setting the bottles and one glass on the coffee table and nudging the other against her shoulder. "Here. Get that down you." She accepted her drink, and I watched her gulp a couple of mouthfuls, wondering what was going on in her head. Did she need a few moments to get herself together after Nessie's interruption, or was she having second thoughts? I knew I was pushing it, but as much as I'd been trying to convince myself to take it slowly, I couldn't. The attraction was there. I knew it. I could feel it. All the signs pointed to it being something real. If she needed time, she could have some.

Sitting on the rug below her, I opened my sketchbook. "What do you think?" I said, holding it out.

After a moment of study, she finally spoke. "What's this?" she asked, pointing to the structure at the side of the pool.

"The pergola we discussed. If you flip the page, I've done a more detailed close-up."

She turned to the next sheet. "I don't remember it being much of a discussion."

"Suggestion then. Don't you like it? Because I can always change it, if you want."

Still studying the picture, she asked, "Can you really do that?"

"What? Change it?"

"Build it."

"I wouldn't have put it there if I couldn't."

"It seems like a lot of work." Cora drained her glass without looking at it, and before she could set it down, I refilled it.

"Nothing's too much trouble for you."

A small smile played across her lips. "The space would be useful, but I can't see how it's going to fit."

I leaned back on the plush pile, resting on my elbows. "Don't worry about that. As soon as I get rid of that old maple tree, there'll be plenty of room."

"Really? You want to get rid of the maple tree? Don't you like it?"

"I'm sure it was great, in its day, but not now. I can always plant a new one somewhere, if it was a favourite of yours."

Finally, she looked down at me. "Is that what you do, get rid of things that are past their prime and replace them with younger models?"

"Ah, I see where you're going with this. Our age difference really is a big thing for you, isn't it?"

Cora glanced at her glass, and noticing it was empty again, she placed it on the carpet at her feet, and sighed.

Despite asking the question, I didn't want to hear the answer, so I changed the subject. "What do you think of the steel waterfall?"

"Huh? Oh." She turned the sketchpad, considering it from different angles. "Is that what that is?"

"If it's not your style, I could always raise the side border and run a rocky waterfall into the swimming pool."

"My home is not a cheap beachside hotel." Her eyes held a glint of distaste.

"I know. That's why I went for the steel. It's modern and beautiful, just like the house's owner."

Cora's attention shifted from the sketch to me. "If that hadn't sounded so cheesy, I might be flattered. It's been a long time since anyone has called me beautiful."

My eyes roved from her red painted toenails up the smooth line of her legs, briefly halted at the enticing shadow cast by the hem of her skirt stretched over her thighs, and stopped at her unusually coloured eyes. Every inch of her was stunning. "Get used to it, because you're going to be hearing it a lot more."

Cora held my gaze, as if daring me to come to my senses, and without looking, she placed the sketchbook on the sofa and pushed off the cushion to kneel next to me. Her hands found the rug at either side of my hips, and her head lowered until our faces were almost touching. "Look at me, Johnny."

"Oh, believe me, I'm looking." I broke her stare, for a second, to scan down her cleavage, before meeting her eyes again.

"No. I mean really look at me. Closely. I have lines around my eyes. They're not going to disappear, and they're getting bigger every day."

She had to be kidding. You'd need a magnifying glass to see her flaws. "You're beautiful."

"And stretch marks, I have those too." She lifted one hand to smooth the side of her breast. "Here." Her hand dropped slowly and stroked across her lower abdomen. "And here."

She must have known what effect it was having. It was as if she were giving me my own personal lap dance. I found her touching herself to be highly erotic, and I longed to reach out and follow her lead. "I don't care."

"They're not beautiful, Johnny."

"Show me."

I hadn't expected her to comply, so I was surprised when she sat back on her heels, lifted the hem of her blouse, and pulled down the waistband of her skirt to expose a tantalizing sliver of stomach. "See. I'm ugly."

I ran my fingers over the faint indents. "I've seen twenty year-old girls with bigger ones than that."

"I don't believe you."

"It's true. I wouldn't have noticed them if you hadn't pointed them out."

The blouse dropped, along with her eyes. "You're just being complimentary to get me into bed."

"No way did you just say that. Is that what you really think?"

"Well aren't you? Isn't sleeping with an older woman not on your mental list of things to do before you're thirty?"

"I don't have a list, but if I did, getting you to like me would be at the top."

"I already like you."

"You have a funny way of showing it."

"I let you kiss me, didn't I?"

"Would you let me do it again?"

"Maybe."

"Now?"

The corners of her mouth crept up. "Maybe."

I sat up and bottom shunted over to her. "I don't do too good with maybes." Leaning on one arm to get as close to her as I could, without us actually touching, I said, "A yes or no will do. Preferably a yes."

Cora's eyes dropped to my mouth and she licked her lips, before nodding slowly. I caressed her cheek with my free hand and angled my head in, stopping short as she bent to meet me, and pulling back. "Are you going to push me away again? Because there's only so much rejection a guy can take."

She let out a small sigh. "I want you to kiss me, Johnny."

Chapter Sixteen

I wanted to kiss her too, badly, but the devil inside me had other ideas. If this was the moment I'd waited for, I wanted to hold on to the anticipation just a little while longer, so I stood up and walked to the corner of the room.

"Where are you going?" Cora asked.

I turned the knob on her ancient stereo stack. "You realise this thing is almost an antique. You should think about updating it to something sleeker, maybe even computerised." Music filled the room. "There're some great integrated sound systems on the market nowadays."

"It was John's. He liked the retro feel. He also liked this track. Could you change it, please? Try number four."

I pushed button four, and a slow song filtered through the speakers. I held out my hands. "Dance?"

With a puzzled expression, she rose to her feet, smoothed down her skirt, and approached me. "You continue to surprise me, Johnny."

My hands crept around her waist. "I aim to please."

She hooked her arms around my neck and laid her head on my shoulder. As we swayed to the music, her fingers played with the curls lying on my nape, and her warm breath heated my neck.

I'd hoped making her wait would get her all hot and panting for me, but she relaxed into my hold and seemed quite content, not flustered at all. On the flip side, I was more than flustered; I was uncomfortable. A few minutes of close contact had me so hard it hurt, and my jeans were in danger of cutting off my blood supply from the waist down. My body's reaction crushed the devil inside, and all thoughts of stalling vanished. I eased away from her and looked deep into her eyes. She reciprocated, making me all warm and fuzzy. An alien feeling, but one I'd be happy to get used to.

No longer able to hold back, I dipped my head and brushed my lips against hers. It amazed me how she yielded to the kiss, slowly increasing the pressure, using her tongue to tease me to distraction. It was only our second kiss, but her mouth was becoming so familiar, it was tempting to devour it all. I didn't want to push her too soon, so I resisted, keeping the pace languid and sensual. Small moans softly purred in her throat, and an intense heat built between us. My hands moved from her waist; one dropping to gently grip her ass, and the other sliding under the cotton fabric of her blouse to follow the dent of her spine up to her bra strap. I itched to snap open the clasp and reach around to her full breasts, but I kept my reserve, hoping she'd allow things to go further this time.

She broke away, and I looked down at her, heart pounding, waiting.

"I haven't done this for a very long time," she said.

"What? Dancing?"

"No." She shook her head. "This."

Comprehension dawned. The light was on amber, about to turn green. But was there some reason she couldn't say the word? Did I have to spell it out? "You mean, sex with someone other than your husband?"

"Sex with anyone."

"Not following."

"Like I said before, John was married to his job. He worked so hard; he was always tired by the time he got home, and his interest in me declined as his responsibilities increased."

"He didn't know a good thing when he had it."

Her eyes filled with sadness. "During our reconciliation, last year, I tried to elicit his interest. I really did, but he always had an excuse."

"And he left you again for another woman."

She nodded into her chest, pointedly avoiding my gaze. "His disinterest convinced me I was undesirable. His unfaithfulness confirmed it."

"Trust me. That is not the case. I've never wanted anyone more." Or hated anyone more than her Ex. It was a crime against mankind for a body like hers not to be touched, and loved, every single day.

"That's what I'm struggling to understand."

I pushed as much sincerity into my eyes as I could. "Cora, I desire you." I took hold of her hand and placed it on my jeans. "Would I have this if I didn't?"

Her eyes widened, and with the lightest of touches, her other hand moved to my shoulder and continued down my arm until we were holding hands. She dropped to her knees, pulling me down with her. "I am tired of being alone," she said. "I want to feel loved again." My heart raced. She had my undivided attention, as she moved to release her blouse's buttons, one by one, and parted the material. "So where were we?"

I didn't need asking twice, and reached up to cup a breast in each hand. "Right about here."

Her eyes closed and she pushed her chest forwards, inviting me to touch her more. I was only too happy to oblige. Through the lacy material, her nipples hardened under the pressure of my rotating thumbs. I leaned in to dot light kisses along her collarbone. Her chest heaved; her breathing laboured. Touching her was better than all my birthdays put together, and her body was the present I was dying to unwrap. I sought her mouth again, as my fingers travelled upwards to bare her shoulders, then moved back down to continue working her newly exposed breasts. It was as if I'd never touched a woman before, exploring curves that were both soft and firm at the same time. She pulled back and fought for air.

"Christ, you drive me crazy," I whispered. "I want to see you naked."

Filled with a mixture of excitement and terror, her eyes flicked to the lamp. "I-I ..."

"It's okay. You don't have to be embarrassed; you have a wonderful body."

She took a deep breath. "You first."

"Suits me." I couldn't shed my clothes quickly enough, and within seconds, I was kneeling in front of her wearing only my boxers. "Bringing back memories?"

"That's not naked."

"Not what you said before." I grinned. "Besides, I wouldn't want to overwhelm you all at once."

"I've seen a naked man before."

Part of me decided I was better off not knowing, but the rest of me had to ask, "How many?"

"Just the one."

"A one-man woman, huh?"

"Until now."

I pulled her to me. "Until now."

Easing off her blouse and unhooking the offending elastic, I uncovered the hottest sight I'd ever seen, but I still needed more. I had to expose every inch of this woman.

I scooped her around the waist and swung her gently to the floor. She giggled and looked at me expectantly, before I bent to nuzzle her neck and trail kisses down between her breasts. As I smoothed a hand down her side and unzipped her skirt, I circled one pink nipple with my tongue, attached my lips around it, and sucked, gently at first then harder. Air pulled through her nose, as her back rose from the floor, allowing me access to nudge the skirt down over her hips, and when my attention switched to her other nipple, her panties followed. She kicked them off with her feet.

Greedily, I scanned down the length of Cora's body. The thought of it had had me all bent out of shape for weeks, and now it was mine for the taking. Skimming her stomach with the lightest of fingertips, I inched lower to my goal, and below her soft curls, I found it. Holy fuck, she was already wet for me. Her fingers teased under the waistband of my boxers, and the sensation of her touching my ass drove me wild, but I knew if my underwear came off, it'd be over in minutes, and I wanted it to be good for her too, besides, I liked to play. I smoothed my finger between her legs and slid inside. She tensed. "Shh. Relax," I said, as I worked in another finger.

"I ..."

"Shh." I silenced any protest, she was about to make, with another kiss, and soon, her hips were mirroring the movement of my fingers, her glorious flesh soft to my touch. She stilled, and I broke away to look down at her closed eyes and ask, "Are you holding your breath?"

Her eyelids flew open. "Shh," she said, glancing down at my hand, "and don't stop."

"I have a better idea," I said, as I began kissing a line down past her belly button. "I want to know if you taste as good as you feel."

A small sound, I couldn't make out, escaped her lips, as I replaced my fingers with my tongue and hooked my arms under her hips. Her thighs parted in open welcome, and I pressed my tongue deep inside her, alternating penetration with lapping and circling her sweet spot. She shivered, and tugged on my hair. Any harder and I'd be balder than Paps. Yeah, baby. I know. I'm good. I usually had to work a pussy for a good ten minutes for it to purr. It took Cora about twenty seconds, before she shuddered and struggled for breath.

I inched back up, and beamed. "Nice, huh?"

"Amazing," she said through ragged breaths.

"And I'm not done with you yet," I said, reaching over her to the pocket of my discarded jeans and retrieving the foil packet. I knelt up and straddled her, whilst ripping the packet open with my teeth. "Now you get to undress me."

She chewed on her bottom lip and ran the back of her forefinger up my length, before hooking her thumbs into my boxers and slipping them down. Her eyes widened as my dick sprang out.

My lip curled into a lopsided smile. "He's all yours. Treat him gently."

I eased down to lie beside her and enveloped her in my arms. She was trembling.

"Why are you nervous?" I asked. "I thought we'd passed that."

"I don't want to disappoint you."

"Not possible. You could lie there like a shop window mannequin and I'd still be happy to be with you. Now, how do you like it?"

She smiled. "Just be you." Her hands reached up to my face and she pulled me into a kiss, as I shifted to position myself between her thighs. With our chests pressed together, I could feel her heart racing against mine. I kissed every part of her within easy reach, taking my time, while my hands explored lower. She needed to be fully ready. Primed. Her flesh felt wonderful under my fingers, every contact heated my blood to boiling point. Finally, she reached between us and guided me in. I almost shot my load right then. It was tempting, and I knew it wouldn't take long for me to be ready for action again, but after all my talk, I had to live up to my promise.

With slow, calculated movements, I pulled out and

pressed back in, again and again. I wanted to stay inside her forever. This was where I belonged. I savoured each second, like I would a freshly blown bubble that could pop and disappear in a flash. Soft moans and tiny sounds broke free from her lips. Perfectly manicured nails raked down my shoulder blades and dug into my clenched ass cheeks. Pain heightened the pleasure, and I fought to hold back as the pressure built. Then just when I thought I couldn't take any more, Cora's back arched, and she tightened around me. She was close. I could feel it. And so was I. I had been since we'd first kissed in the kitchen, and the wait was agony. When the first shudder rippled through her, I finally let go and came harder than I ever had before.

Chapter Seventeen

I woke up with a huge grin firmly fixed on my face. Cora was facing me, watching me intently. Over her shoulder, the clock had already crept past ten. My smile widened, as I remembered the previous night. Somewhere between the third and fourth time, we'd made it into the bedroom. "Morning, beautiful. Sleep well?" I asked.

"Very," she said.

"Me too." I noticed her face held a tinge of sadness. "So, what's wrong?"

"Nothing."

"Don't give me that. I'm not totally blind."

She chewed on her bottom lip, and then sighed. "Last night was really special."

I got the feeling she was about to come out with one of her 'buts'. "It was mind blowing."

"Yes. But you do know it can never be anything more than that. Just one incredible night."

And there was the 'but'. "What are you saying?"

"It was a mistake."

I ran my fingers down her arm, and I let my hand rest on her waist. "No. No, it wasn't. It was a good thing."

"We got caught up in the moment. It was sexual chemistry. That's all."

"There's nothing wrong with a bit of chemistry."

"No. No, there isn't. But it never lasts."

"And you're basing this on what … your vast experience?"

"Clearly not. But Diane—"

"Is not you. Are you telling me, in the cold light of day, you don't want me anymore?"

Her gaze fell, as if she couldn't bear to look me in the eye. "No. No, that's not what I'm saying."

Thank fuck for that. "Pleased to hear it. What then?"

"When I'm with you, I forget I'm not twenty anymore."

Were we really back to this? "When I'm with you, it doesn't occur to me that you're not."

"But it's a fact. You can't ignore it. I'm thirty-nine; you're only twenty-two."

"Twenty-three in September."

"Upping one number doesn't change the others." She twisted her wedding ring, and I had the sudden desire to rip it from her finger and throw it across the room.

"Quit with the old lady bullshit, will you?"

I half expected her to chastise me for my outburst, but instead, she glanced up through her lashes with an expression so pained it knotted my heart. "It's not just about age. There's a world of difference between us. We can't base a relationship on chemistry alone."

"It's a start. What's the harm in giving it a shot?"

"I don't know if I'm ready," she said.

"Why?"

"I'm scared."

Again? If she thought being with me was scary, she must have led a very sheltered life. "Of what?"

"Of what people will say, of getting too attached and you leaving me, of being hurt again."

"Fuck what anyone else thinks. This is about us." I hooked a finger under her chin and forced her to look at me. "Look, no one can ever predict whether a relationship will work out or not. It's not an exact science, but I'm willing to take the risk. The question is, are you?" I tried to gauge her reaction, but her face remained rigid, so I pressed harder. "I'm not going to hurt you. But neither will I allow you to give up on us before we've even started. Not when I feel this way, and I think you feel it too. You do don't you?"

Her head bobbed, almost indistinguishably. "You make me happy, happier than I've been in a long time."

"And I wish that everyone could experience a mere scrap of what I feel for you. I've never felt this way about a woman before. I'm putting myself out there too, but we have to give this a shot. We deserve it. You deserve it. It's time to stop taking care of everyone else and let me take care of you." It was the first time I'd given such a pussy speech, but I felt as if I was hanging on to our time by my fingernails, and I needed to get a firm grip.

Her chest depressed as she forced out a breath. "How can you take care of me? You don't even have a job."

"I'm not talking about finances, woman. I'm talking about your needs. My needs. I need to be with you, make you feel good. And you have to admit we're good together."

"Yes, but we have nothing in common."

"Of course, we do. You like to keep fit. So do I. You like baking. I like eating. We're both alone. The rest we'll work out. All I'm asking is that you give it a try."

"I want to try. It's just …"

"You have trust issues. I get that. But you can trust me. I promise. I'll never lie to you, and I'll never cheat on you, like your Ex did, but you have to let me be in your life. Okay?" She had to agree. No way could I go back to mowing her lawns and pretend our time together never happened. I held my breath, my whole body taught with fear, as I waited for her answer.

"Yes."

"Yes?"

She nodded. "Yes."

The tension in my stomach finally eased and allowed me to breathe again. "That settles it then. Now come here." I reached behind her neck and pulled her lips to mine. My fear of losing her had to be greater than hers was of losing me. The relief of her answer brought tears to my eyes, and I poured all my emotion into our kiss, afraid to let her go in case she changed her mind. After a few seconds, I managed to regain my self-control and broke contact. "Thank you."

She smiled. The kind of smile I'd only ever dreamt about. Hell, if this was what love felt like, sign me up.

"So, how are you feeling?" I asked.

The corners of her lips curled mischievously. "Sore."

"Yeah?" Not too sore, I hoped. Despite repeated performances throughout the evening, I'd woken up hard, and the way she was looking at me did nothing to lesson it. Last night had been a revelation. I'd expected it would take time for Cora to be at ease with me, but I'd been surprised at her eagerness. I was ready for another round, if she was game.

"Yes. It's been a long time since I've had carpet burns on my knees," Cora said.

"Carpet burns? Really? Let's see them, then." I scooted under the sheet and kissed my way down the side of her ribcage to her legs. She squirmed and giggled. I hadn't quite reached her knees when I heard the bedroom door open.

Were we in for another rant from Nessie? Because I could do without one of her angry outbursts cramping my style, yet again.

"Mum?" said a voice that sounded like Nessie's, but wasn't. I froze. "I came round to collect some more of my stuff, and then I heard noises. I ..." My fringe tickled my nose and I sneezed. "Is that ... Dad, under there?"

Cora peeled the sheet from my head, and I turned to the voice. It belonged to another mini Cora. "Hi," I said.

"Oh. Um, hello," the girl replied. "I'm sorry, Mum. I didn't know you had company."

Although her tone held a trace of shock, it made a welcome change from her sister's usual loathing. I did a quick top to toe of Cora's eldest, as I shuffled to a sitting position. Her blonde hair fell in waves over a huge rack, squeezed into a tight yellow top, and skintight jeans covered the longest legs I'd ever seen. I found myself wondering if Cora had looked as hot, twenty years ago, then kicked myself. She was still hot, and she was mine. My eyes were under a strict no wandering order now, especially where her daughters were concerned.

"Amy, this is Johnny. My, um ..." Cora began.

Yes, what was I? Gardener? Handyman? Neither sounded right in the current situation. "Boyfriend." I interrupted. Amy's eyebrows rose and she shot a look at her mother. I turned to look at Cora too. "Right?"

Cora's eyes flicked nervously between us. She opened her mouth, and I could tell her brain was struggling to find a plausible alternative. Finally, she spoke, "Yes."

"Okay. Um. I'm not sure quite how to respond to that. You never told me you were seeing anyone, Mum."

"It's been a recent development," Cora said.

"I see. Hmm. Well ... congratulations."

I took hold of Cora's hand and squeezed it, smiling. "Thank you. We're very happy."

Amy's lips twitched into a smile. "Mum deserves to be happy." Her gaze roamed over my chest and back to my eyes. Was she checking me out? "Are you older than you look?" she asked. "Yeah, I'm guessing you must be," she said, answering her own question. "Well, I'll just get my things, and then I'll be out of your hair. Nice to meet you, Johnny. Mum, I'll call you later."

When the door closed, I turned to Cora. "That went well, I think."

She was staring at me with raised brows. "Boyfriend?"

"You like that?"

"It sounded strange."

"What would you prefer? Partner?" I shook my head. "Too formal. Bit on the side? Implies you already have somebody. Shag buddy? Well, as much as that idea appeals, we've already established it's more than that. Personally, I like boyfriend, and as far as I'm concerned, we're a couple

---

141

now. So, boyfriend it is. What shall we do today?" I asked, closing the space between us and kissing her shoulder.

"It's Friday. On Fridays, I have yoga class in the morning, go shopping in the afternoon, and host my book club in the evening. In fact, my class starts at eleven, so I really need to get ready," she said, opening the space back up.

"Are you trying to get rid of me?"

"Yes."

I shuffled closer and ran my tongue along the edge of her ear. "Why?"

Using more force, she pushed me away and swung her legs off the mattress. "You're far too tempting."

"Okay, I can take a hint. I was thinking of going into town anyway."

♠ ♠ ♠

Chapter Eighteen

Once the new haircut had been ticked off my mental list, I paid a visit to the job centre, hoping to find someone in need of an odd job man. I was out of luck. Row upon row of white cards pinned to billboards offered a variety of menial positions: shop work, cleaning, labouring stuff, but no demand for gardeners. The school caretaker job half appealed—at least the pay did—but scraping chewing gum from desks and fixing toilets in graffiti covered bathrooms wasn't my scene, and I wasn't yet desperate enough to flip burgers or collect glasses. I scanned the depressing, soulless room of blank faces holding no hope and couldn't get out of there soon enough.

Feeling frustrated and defeated, I decided to hold on to my bus fare and walk the short distance home. At this rate, it would take years to get enough cash together for the land. My journey took me past the police station, and I was so preoccupied with wondering how the fuck I was going to boost my bank balance, that my eyes were fixed on the pavement instead of the way ahead, and I had to stop abruptly when a captive was hauled from the back of a Black Maria and across my path. As I watched the men disappear through the door, a poster in the window caught my attention.

It was a notice asking for volunteers to help tidy up the local cemetery. They were after free labour, but hey, I didn't mind giving up my time, and if it helped get the word out, I could write it off as advertising. I called inside and picked up an information leaflet from the desk.

I arrived home to the sound of indie rock. Kendrick was in the living room, and he wasn't alone. He was with a girl— and a pretty one at that, if you discounted the bruises on her face. He glanced up as I entered, and sniggered. "Fuck me. Finally found the scissors, huh? About time."

"You like? I asked, ruffling my fingers across what was left of my hair.

"Looking sharp, dude." He pushed out his bottom lip as his head bobbed. "So, where were you, last night? Your bed wasn't slept in."

"Next door."

"All night?"

"I was kinda busy."

"Yeah, but all night, dude? What did you do, fall asleep in the shed? I thought you'd finished there?"

"Man, I've only just started. Where's Paps?"

"Taking a nap."

I glanced at the empty chair in the corner. "Where?"

"Upstairs."

Right on cue, the muffled sound of coughing sounded from above. "It's not like him to take to his bed. Is he okay?"

Kendrick shrugged. "Looked fine to me. I guess he didn't want to intrude. Stop changing the subject."

"What subject?"

"Where the fuck were you ... exactly?"

I took Pappa's spot in his chair and stretched out my legs. Smokey interrupted his snooze on the hearth rug to offer me a disapproving stare, before licking his lips and resuming his catnap. "Don't worry. Your dibs are still intact," I said, smiling at the girl. "Are you going to introduce me?"

He took hold of the girl's hand, squeezed it, and grinned. "This is my friend, Molly."

"Hi," I said. "I'm Johnny, an older version of this dipshit." I nodded at my brother.

Molly managed to force out a barely audible hello, before Kendrick explained, "She needs a place to stay tonight."

"You mean you need a place to stick your dick."

"Hey! Watch your mouth. It's not like that. Molly's a friend."

"You don't have *girl* friends."

"I do now."

Molly pulled her hand from Kendrick's and fidgeted, nervously. "Perhaps I'd better go."

Kendrick laid a hand on her thigh. "You're going nowhere," he said.

"I don't want to intrude."

Something about the girl prodded my freak out cells. She looked too much of a mouse to be one of Kendrick's usual no strings bimbos. And what was with her fucked-up face? Maybe she wasn't as innocent as she looked, and Kendrick's gentlemanly ruse was all a plan to get his leg over later. Yeah, that must be it, unless I didn't know my brother as well as I thought I did.

"Bollocks to that. Like I said, I'm fine with the sofa."

"She can take my bed. I'm sleeping out." At least, that was the plan.

"Again? Where this time?"

"Same place."

"Have you developed a thing for spiders?"

"No. For Cora." I pulled a menu from under the telephone on Pappa's table. "Should we order takeout? We can get extra for when Paps wakes up."

"Back up a second. What did you say?"

Here we go. Take a deep breath, Johnny, and just come out with it. It's not like you're keeping it a secret. "I was with Cora, last night."

"What do you mean, with her?"

"You need me to draw you a picture?"

"Are you yanking my chain?"

"Nope."

"I thought you were joking when you staked a claim."

"Never been more serious."

Kendrick's creased brow ironed out as his lips curled to a smile. "My brother the perv."

"Says the guy who was checking her out, which, by the way, you can quit now."

"I admit she has a rocking body, but there's a big difference between looking and touching."

"Yeah, there is," I said with a huge grin.

Kendrick's mouth fell open. "Jesus, man, you've slammed her already, haven't you?"

"Well, we weren't playing Monopoly."

"Are you out of your mind?"

"Only if you count being crazy about her."

"Crazy's right. What are you going to do now? Move in? Buy a sedan? Play daddy?"

Talking about Cora only made me long to be with her. "Don't be stupid. It's too soon for that, but I really like her, man. I think I've found the woman I want to spend the rest of my life with."

"Dude, I reckon you need your rocks feeling, but what do I know? Have your kicks, if you must, but don't expect any double dates. I've my street cred to consider."

♠ ♠ ♠
Chapter Nineteen

I didn't bother knocking, and I was about to call out Cora's name when I heard voices in the living room. Her book club. Shit. I'd completely forgotten she would have visitors. Still, it couldn't go on all night. I clicked the door latch into place, as quietly as possible, and tiptoed along the corridor to the kitchen to wait it out, but I'd forgotten about Cora's open-plan layout and had to duck down behind the separating breakfast bar, before anyone saw me.

On the table, numerous plates were laid out with tiny square sandwiches and miniature cakes. Cora had been busy. Four bottles of wine sat on the counter next to a cluster of empty glasses, and an enticing aroma drifted from the coffee machine. Despite wolfing down a twelve-inch pizza only an hour before, my stomach rumbled eagerly.

"You were supposed to read the book, Sheila. Watching the film doesn't count." The voice belonged to Cora's friend, Diane.

"I know. I know. It's no excuse, but I've just been so busy this week."

"Why? Have you found a lover?" Diane asked with a low drawl.

"Unlike you, some of us have a husband and children. I don't expect a single woman to understand the responsibilities that entails."

"And I don't wish to."

"Perhaps we should take a break," Cora suggested. "We can discuss the underlying themes to the story after we've had some refreshments."

Refreshments? Damn. Did that mean they'd be coming into the kitchen? I'd look a right Charlie, hiding on the floor, if that happened. If I was quick, I might have time to sneak back out of the door. I glanced down at the white shirt and black trousers I'd chosen to wear for the evening, and saw the opportunity to have some fun instead, so I crawled around the tiles on my hands and knees, pulled the tea towel from a hook near the sink, laid it over my arm, and grabbed a bottle of wine from the counter as I stood.

"I'll take that as my cue, ladies. Wine or coffee?"

A circle of shocked faces stared over to me. The one seated next to Cora spoke. "You hired help, Cora? How very grandiose of you," she said, looking me up and down.

Cora's mouth formed an O, but no words came out.

With an aloof air, I strolled into the seating area and prised myself into the circle of bodies to place a handful of glasses on the coffee table.

"This certainly adds spice to the evening," another woman added, winking at me.

I smiled back. "I'm just here to serve the refreshments, madam."

"That's a shame," Diane said. "I'm a good tipper."

"Yeah, I bet you are," I said through a half grin.

An arm waved at the edge of my vision. "I'll take some of what you're offering, sweetie."

Jeez, the women were like a herd of hungry hippos waiting to devour me. Maybe, I hadn't thought this through.

As I poured more wine, Cora finally found her voice. "The usual nibbles are in the kitchen. Perhaps you'd like to help yourselves," she said, speaking to the room. The women rose, and Cora smiled at each one as they passed by, before turning to me and whispering, "What are you doing here, Johnny?"

"Don't you want me to meet your friends?"

"Eventually, perhaps, but not yet. It's too soon," she said through gritted teeth.

"So I'm to be your dirty little secret?" I jiggled my eyebrows and sneakily kissed her cheek.

She jumped and stole a quick glance at the women. She was safe. No one had noticed, but the woman I guessed to be Sheila—she was the only one not giving me sideways looks—was making her way back to the sofa, carrying a plate of sandwiches. I offered her a glass of wine and a smile.

"Thank you," she said. Yep. Her voice confirmed my suspicions. Definitely Sheila. She accepted the glass and sat down. "I saw Madeleine today, Cora."

A sudden chill filled the air. "And?"

"I thought you might like to know."

"Why? I have no interest in that woman anymore."

Not wanting to be the third wheel in the conversation, I gave a cursory nod and left them alone, but I couldn't help keeping one ear in the room.

"Not even if she was with another man? One that wasn't John. They looked pretty cosy."

"Try the brownies," I said to the brunette at my side. "I personally recommend them."

"Well, if you insist," she answered, looking up through her lashes and nibbling the side of her lip. I smiled weakly.

"What are you getting at, Sheila?" Cora's voice rose slightly.

"Only that John might be available again ... if you wanted him back, that is."

Fuck that. No way. He'd had his chance and blown it. Cora belonged to me now.

"Why would I want that?"

"You were happy before."

Was she?

"I was … for a while, before he changed."

"You could be happy again."

"Not with a dirty, cheating scumbag."

That's right, Cora. You tell it like it is.

"Aw, come on. You're not the solitary type. You need man to take care of."

She has one.

"I have one," Cora said in a matter-of-fact way that surprised me.

I nodded to myself with more than a hint of satisfaction.

"You do? You've been keeping that tasty piece of news a secret. Who is he?" Sheila asked.

Diane shimmied past me and returned to her friends. "Is it Roger? I mean, I know you said the date didn't work out, but I knew he'd be perfect for you."

"My goodness. No. It isn't Roger."

"Who then?"

"You don't know him."

"Okay. When do we get to meet him?" Diane asked.

Cora stole a glance in my direction. "It's early days. Let's just see how it goes."

"Why the secrecy? You know I'm going to get the juicy details from you eventually."

Cora caught my eye. "Could I possibly have a top up, please?"

I made my way back to the sofa, as Sheila pointed to her plate. "Mmm, these are delicious. You'll have to give me the recipe, Cora." She smacked her lips as she rose from her chair and squeezed past me. "I think I'll just get one more slice."

Diane bottom shuffled along the sofa and closed in on Cora. "Okay," she spoke softly to Cora's cheek. "Who he is can wait. Start with how hot his body is and what he does with it."

"Just because you enjoy telling me about your sex life doesn't mean you get to know about mine," Cora said.

"Spoilsport."

"Excuse me, ladies." I squeezed between them, to pour Cora's wine and couldn't resist giving her a cheeky wink. Her eyes smiled back, even though the corners of her mouth resisted.

Diane gasped. "I saw that."

"What?"

"Don't play the innocent with me. I'm your best friend. I know you better than anyone, and I know men even better." Diane looked up at me through narrowed eyes. "It's you." She whirled to face Cora again. "It is, isn't it? It's him! I should have been suspicious from the start. You've never hired help for one of our evenings before."

"His name's Johnny."

I lifted the bottle in greeting. "Hi."

"Nice to meet you, Johnny, but let's get serious." She turned back to Cora. "You haven't thought this through, darling. I'm all for you having another man in your life. Heck, I encouraged it. But Johnny is not that man. He's barely grown into the description, yet. Look, I can imagine how it must feel to have someone so young and virile in your bed. It's not as if it hasn't been a fantasy of mine too, but he's not relationship material. Life doesn't work that way."

"Oh? How does life work, Diane? Is there a plan I should be following?"

"I understand your fears. You're pushing forty and you think you're running out of time. It happens to all of us."

"You're talking about me as if I'm a discarded woman, tossed on the junk heap of life like last year's Gucci handbag."

"I happen to like vintage," I cut in. "Just because there's a newer model on the market, doesn't mean it's more useful or attractive. Beauty changes over time; it never lessens, and a classic model is a keeper." The way Cora smiled at my words proved my point. I caught Diane with a challenging stare. "Stop trying to find problems where there aren't any."

Diane's voice rose along with her frustration. "Cora, you can't recapture your youth by trawling the schoolyard for a date."

Over exaggerate much? "Do I look like a schoolboy?" I asked.

Diane ignored my question, as Cora said, "Keep your voice down, Diane. I don't want all the girls knowing yet, and I didn't go trawling anywhere. In case you haven't noticed, Johnny's been working in the garden, and he pursued me."

"And you were flattered. Who wouldn't have been?"

"It's more than that. I never thought I'd find someone who would make me feel like this. I have returned to the land of the living, which is what you've been pressing me for, for months. Can't you just be happy for me?"

"I would, if I thought for one second it wasn't doomed. He's going to leave you, darling. Maybe not tomorrow or next week, but someday, when he finds someone younger and more … flexible. Don't think for a minute he won't. Is that not something that's ever entered your head?"

I placed the bottle a little too heavily onto the coffee table. "Hey. I'm standing right here. Stop filling her head with ridiculous ideas."

"Please, Cora. Think this through. End it now, before he does, and hold on to a modicum of self-respect."

"You're jealous. That's it, isn't it? All the men you date are stuffy and old."

Diane dismissed Cora's comment with a shake of her head. "Johnny, let me ask you something. What do you see in Cora?"

"Diane, that's not fair. You don't have to answer that, Johnny."

"No, it's okay. I've got this." I looked Diane square in the eye. "I admit, I first fell for her hot body, but she's also kind, and gentle, and funny. She doesn't take shit, but she does it with class. She looks after herself, and everyone else, and she's exactly the sort of woman any man would be lucky to have."

"Precisely. Why should that be you?"

"Because, despite your opinion, our love is real."

♠ ♠ ♠

Chapter Twenty

I wiped the sweat from my forehead and stabbed the shovel into the earth. Cora was topping up her tan on a nearby lounger.

Using the word love hadn't been planned. Perhaps it was too soon to be mentioned, but it was how I felt, and once it was out there, there was no going back. A tingle still ran through me when I remembered Cora's reaction. She hadn't commented. Her sweet face had spoken for her, and I was convinced she would say the words, when she was ready.

I looked over to her. She wriggled in her seat, looking anything but relaxed, chewing on her bottom lip and staring into a gin and tonic.

Some of Nessie's belongings had disappeared the previous day, while Cora was out jogging, but Nessie wasn't answering the texts or calls Cora made, and if she didn't stop worrying over her daughter's absence, I'd soon be able to plant seeds in her frown lines. It felt as if everything was my fault, and I wished I could make it better. Why couldn't Nessie just accept the situation, like her sister, Amy, had?

"Have you tried calling Jess?" I asked, peeling off my T-shirt. Dang, the day was far too hot to be digging.

Cora's eyes grazed over my abs. "Do you think I should?"

"It's gotta be worth a shot."

"Yes. Yes, you're right." She placed her glass on the table beside her, picked up her phone, and tapped on the keypad.

I returned my attention to the shovel, but couldn't face picking it up again. It was time for a break, and on a day like this, there was only one kind. I stripped down to my boxers, took a run-up, and dived into the pool.

Soft water rippled over my aching muscles, instantly cooling me to the core. In the blue of the underwater cocoon, life was clean and shiny and crammed with sparkles. If only it were really like that. When you're starting out on life's big fishing trip, no one tells you the freaking river of life is full of sewage and the weeds will try to pull you under.

It had been a pretty busy week, all told. I'd started work on the old cemetery, and that had led to a couple of one-off jobs for some local old folk, but I'd spent every spare moment I had with Cora, both in her garden and her bed.

Reaching the other end of the pool, I took a quick breath as I turned around, and swam back towards Cora. When I surfaced, I was staring at her crotch. She was sitting on the edge of the pool, swirling her feet through the waves. Her bikini bottoms were stretched tight, moulding over her curls, and my body responded to the sight. We'd made love every single day, sometimes more than once, and I still couldn't get enough of her sizzling hot body.

Dragging my eyes up to hers, I asked, "Any luck?"

"Vanessa's in Ireland."

"She's where?"

"Ireland, the large piece of land off the west coast."

"I know where Ireland is. What is she doing there?"

"Spending time with her boyfriend. He lives there."

"Oh. I didn't know that. Does Jess have any idea when she might be coming back?"

"No, but she never stays long. Garrett's on the road a lot." I must have looked puzzled, as Cora went on to explain, "He manages a band."

"Really? Anyone I've heard of?"

"Now, how would I know that?"

I laid my hands on her thighs and stroked the inside of them with my thumbs. "I guess we still have a lot to learn about each other."

Cora held her face up to the sun. "Vanessa told me who they were, once, and I googled them. They're quite successful, but I can't say I've been interested enough to remember the name." She licked a film of sweat from her top lip and blew her breath up her face.

"Well then. I guess she's safe, and she'll come home when she's ready. So, how about you keep me company in this pool?" My hands moved around to her ass, and I scooped her towards the water. She giggled and wrapped her legs around my waist, before lowering her head to meet my eager lips. The taste of salty sweat mixed with my chlorine flavoured tongue. I pressed her up against the pool edge, pushed her bikini top to the side, and grabbed a handful of creamy flesh. "Have you ever made love in the pool?"

"You are joking?"

"I never joke about pleasure."

"But the neighbours …" She panted.

"Pappa hasn't been outside for days, and the couple at the other side are at work. No one's gonna see."

"You're a wicked man, Johnny."

❀ ❀ ❀

I swam over to where Cora's bikini floated and threw it back to her, before retrieving my boxers and pulling them back on. By the time I swam back to the steps, Cora had dressed.

"I need to take a shower," she said. "I'm meeting Diane for lunch."

I pulled her back as she tried to leave. "Can't you cancel? I'd booked you in for full day's services today," I said with a cheeky grin.

"Aren't I the lucky one?"

I kissed her neck and nibbled playfully on her earlobe. "You don't know how many times you might have been, unless you stay."

"As tempting an offer as that is," she said, pushing me away, "I wouldn't want to keep you from your work. Your client is expecting a professional job."

"Aw, come on. Break the habit of a lifetime. The world won't end if you don't stick to your routine, and my *client* will understand. Stay."

"I've got to go." She kissed me on the cheek, climbed the steps, and grabbed her phone on the way to the house. I watched her dripping ass all the way inside, before climbing out and getting my head back on the job.

♠ ♠ ♠
Chapter Twenty-One

Later that afternoon, I heard Cora's car pull into the driveway. One day I would own a car like hers: a sleek, gas-guzzling, engine purring, look at me I've made it, machine. But the way things were going, that day was a long way off. I'd already had to dip into my savings, this week. Travelling by bus just wasn't working out, and I'd given in and bought myself a truck. It was far from the cutest dog in the pound, but it should be good for a couple more years.

My stomach growled, despite having returned to Pappa's for lunch. I wondered if I should pop home to check in on him again. When I'd seen him earlier, he was sitting in his chair, alternately puffing on his pipe and wheezing.

"I think you should see someone, Paps," I'd said. "You've not been right for days."

"Nothing wrong with me that a break from this damn heat won't cure. My plants would be happier too."

"I'll stick the hose on them later. Can I get you something to eat?"

"Already eaten. Just see to yourself." He'd racked up a lungful of tar, and grumbled, "Damn cough."

"Okay. Drink then?"

"No. Nothing, thank you." Irritation had crept into his voice.

"Are you sure you're okay? You don't look too good."

He'd laughed—an alien sound of late. "I haven't looked like Cary Grant for forty years. Old age will creep up on you too, you know. I'm fine. When I'm dead, you'll know about it."

I worried about Paps. Seventy-six wasn't that old, but the jovial, old man, I'd returned home from uni to, had transformed into a grumpy sod, complaining about the smallest of things, and the new model seemed smaller, whiter. Maybe he just needed to get out in the sun more, instead of avoiding it.

I stared into the hole awaiting the new maple tree, hoping that Cora would think to bring me out a sandwich. She often brought me a bite to keep me going, and now would have been a good time for her to show up with the goods.

A car door slammed, as I dragged the tree into position. Was she going out again, without even saying a hello, or a goodbye? Perhaps she'd been shopping and needed a hand to bring her purchases inside. She'd been gone for hours, and I'd missed the hell out of her. If she were going out again, I couldn't let her disappear without at least a kiss to stoke the fire.

Wiping my hands on my shorts, I headed for the house, but when I reached the back door, I paused. Cora was inside, and she wasn't alone.

"You're looking good, Cora." It was a man's voice.

"Why are you here, John?" That bastard? Seriously? Yes, why was he here? Cora must have been out of her mind to open the door to him. He'd better fuck the hell off, and soon.

"I missed you."

Yeah right.

"Oh really?"

"Have you missed me?"

My body tensed as I waited for her to respond.

"Not for a minute," she shot back.

"I don't believe you."

"Believe what you want."

"Honey, I wish I could fix what I've done. I know it was my fault."

The sound of him using an endearment made me want to punch my fist through the door. I had to see what was going down, so I ducked under the window and peered up over the ledge. The pair were facing each other over the breakfast bar.

"You're damn right it was your fault," Cora said.

"We had a good thing and I threw it away. I'm so sorry."

Did he really believe he could come crawling back into her life, again, with an apology and a smile?

"It's too late to be sorry."

"Don't say that. We can try again."

"Not this time."

"Why not? You took me back before." He rounded the breakfast bar, backing Cora into a corner by the table.

She dodged past him. "I was a fool. I'm not a fool anymore."

"It'll be different this time," he said following her.

"I remember you saying the same thing the last time. It was a lie then and it's a lie now."

"It isn't. Madeleine and I are over. I know what I want now." He took another step forwards, and his line of sight almost connected with mine. I shot back under the sill with my heart beating rapidly.

"The funny thing is, John, so do I. I should have been broken-hearted when you left me for a second time, but I wasn't. I was relieved. Things were never the same between us. We can't get back what we had, and recently, I've realised I don't want to. I'm a different woman to the one you knew. Times change and people move on. I've moved on. You're part of my past. I can't change that, and I wouldn't, but you are no longer part of my future."

A speech like that should have gained John's full attention. I risked another peek.

"Is there someone else?" John paused and studied Cora's face. "That's it, isn't it?"

She avoided his gaze and pushed a strand of hair behind her ear, her trademark sign of nerves. It killed me to witness her discomfort. If she didn't get rid of this asshole soon, I would have no option but to interfere.

"All I'll say is that I'm happier than I've ever been."

A smug smile spread across my face.

"Who is he?"

"None of your business."

"Get rid of him."

What the fuck?

Her eyes flashed back to his. "Excuse me?"

I'd heard enough. My territorial instinct took over. She might not have said it yet, but Cora loved me. John was history, and if he wasn't getting the message from Cora, he'd get it from me, loud and clear.

Attempting to get my wave of emotions under control, I flung open the door and strode into the room. "I think it's time you left."

John eyed me from top to toe and back again. "Who are you to tell me to leave my own house?"

"I'm sorry. I was under the impression you didn't live here anymore."

"Johnny, this is between me and John. Go back outside, please."

I could see Cora was struggling to remain calm, and she was doing a far better job than I was. "I can't believe you're giving this shit the time of day."

"We have history. He's the father of my children. Haven't you got a tree to plant?"

I walked over and placed my body between them. "I don't trust him, and I'm not leaving you alone with him."

John's eyes narrowed as he watched our altercation. "If I wasn't so disgusted by the thought, I'd say there was something more than gardening going on here."

"What if there is?" Cora's voice vibrated my left eardrum. "My private life has nothing to do with you any longer."

"He's a child, Cora."

Audacity puffed out my chest, and I faced up to him. "Oh yeah? If I'm such a child, why don't you show me how much of a man you are?"

He stepped back in disgust. "You think you can compete with me? Look at you." His gaze fell and rose. "You're dropping dirt all over the floor, and do you even own a shirt? Cora, how could you choose a manual labourer, who probably has so few brain cells they get lost swimming around in his head trying to find a friend, over me?"

"Actually, Johnny is very smart, and talented, and exciting," Cora paused to offer the final blow, "and ten times the lover you ever were."

John blew out a breath. "You don't even like sex," he scoffed.

"How would you know?"

"Well, let's see. How about the amount of times I've heard, 'Well, if you must, but make it quick and pull my nightdress back down when you've finished.' Remember those nights?"

"I wish I didn't, but I'm doing my best to forget." Bitterness oozed through her voice.

John's eyes narrowed. "Were you really surprised I looked elsewhere? Being in bed with you was like sleeping with an ice cube."

"Maybe if you'd treated me like a real woman instead of a trophy wife ..."

Thinking about them together made me sick, and hearing him call Cora an ice cube was just ridiculous. If only he knew. "If you want my opinion ..."

John interrupted before I could finish. "You don't get an opinion," he said, roughly pushing me against the lip of the tabletop. The bastard was seriously asking for it. His tone changed, and he reached for Cora's waist. "If sex is what you want, then there's even more of a reason for us to get back together. We had fun, back in the day.

Remember when we were first married? It could be like that again."

Ugh.

"You were a different man then." Thankfully, she smacked his hands and backed away, before I hit more than his hands. "Leave me alone, John. It's over."

With one final scowl, he swung round and stormed off down the corridor. "Fine. Keep your plaything, but don't come crawling back to me when you come to your senses," he shouted.

Cora screamed at his back. "Don't worry. I won't."

I waited for the sound of the front door slamming before taking Cora into my arms. She was shaking. I held her tightly and stroked her hair until she calmed. "It's okay," I said. "He's gone, and now he knows the score, I don't think he'll be back."

She pulled away and looked at me. "I hope not. I don't think I can go through that again."

"You won't have to. If he ever shows his face here again, he's toast."

She sighed and stroked my cheek. "I've tried so hard to put my marriage behind me. I just want to stop fighting old ghosts and live again."

"And you will." I kissed her on the nose and grinned. "Listen. I have an idea."

Her eyebrows pushed together. "What kind of an idea?"

"A really bad one."

"I'm not sure I like the sound of that."

"Do you own a pair of jeans?"

"What are you going to do, make an effigy of John and burn it on a bonfire?"

Now there was a thought. "Um, no. I'd like you to wear them when I pick you up tonight. I have to go home to check on Paps and make sure he gets a decent meal in him, first, but I'll be back around eight."

"Where are we going?"

"It's a surprise."

Chapter Twenty-Two

My jaw almost hit the porch floor when Cora opened the door. "Wow. You're stunning." I'd asked her to wear jeans, thinking dressing down would help her blend in more, but add the fuck-me heels and tight tank, squeezing her tits into perfect mounds at the neckline, and you had a homing beacon for every schmuck with a pair of eyes and a dick. "I'm not sure my knuckles are primed enough to beat off the competition."

"Is it too much? Do I look like mutton? Should I change?" she asked, fondling one of her huge, hooped earrings and glancing down at her outfit. "Yes. I'll go and change. I don't know what I was thinking." She turned to go back inside.

I snagged her arm. "No. Don't. You look fantastic. Nice t ... top."

"It's Amy's."

"It's hot."

"Thank you. Are you going to tell me where we're going now?"

"You'll see."

❀ ❀ ❀

The light was fading by the time we walked the short distance to the Pocket Scratcher. Cora began fidgeting as soon as we passed through the door.

"I'm not sure about this. It looks a bit rough," she said.

"It's a lot rough, and way out of your comfort zone, I'm guessing. That's why I brought you. You said you wanted to live a little."

She coughed. "Live. Yes. Not die," she said, holding tightly to my arm and walking a pace behind me all the way to the bar.

Her eyes darted nervously into every smoky corner, as I ordered a couple of Buds, before studying the bottle I passed her. "What's this?"

"Beer. Don't tell me you've never tried one?"

"No. Actually, I haven't"

I shook my head, laughing. "Then here begins the first lesson."

"Don't I get a glass?"

"Nope. Just wrap those pretty lips of yours around the rim and chug it down your throat."

After a small hesitation, she did as I instructed, and I watched, mesmerised, switching my weight from one leg to the other, when my dick registered the movement of her mouth around the bottle's neck. Receiving a blow job was definitely on the agenda, tonight. She wasn't even breaking to take a breath.

I gestured to Pete for another round, as the track on the jukebox changed, and Cora's knee dipped to the beat of the music.

She placed her empty bottle on the bar. "This takes me back," she said. "I haven't heard this song in years." She swayed, and flung her head from side to side, her blonde locks swishing in time to the tune. I'd never seen anything so sexy in my life.

I gestured for another round. Then picking up the drinks in one hand, I grabbed her hand with my other. "Come on." I'd spotted a free table in the corner, and you had to get in quick when opportunity struck.

"Where are we going?"

"To start living."

I spent the next hour trying to teach Cora how to play pool, and I wouldn't be adding it to my list of successes any time soon. Still, it was worth it. The feel of her ass, wrapped tight under denim, nestling into my crotch as I bent over her to guide her shots, drove me wild. I couldn't wait to get her home and do it minus the denim.

Towards the end of the lesson, the familiar face of a local policeman appeared at my side.

"Missed you at the cemetery today, bud," he said.

"Yeah, sorry. I had another job."

He took a sip of his beer, and cocked his head, eying up Cora's cleavage as she lined up a shot. "No worries. It's almost done anyway."

I waved Cora over, after she almost jabbed the tip of her cue into the baize. "Babe, come and meet a friend of mine."

She straightened up and smiled weakly. "Hello Matthew."

He greeted her with a nod. "Cora."

"You two know each other?"

"A long time," Cora said. "Matthew is Sheila's son. He dated Vanessa for a while."

My brows shot up. "Is that right? I reckon you deserve a medal for that one, mate." I slapped his shoulder playfully.

An uncomfortable silence grew, as Matt's eyes flicked from me to Cora and back again. "So you two are … um …"

"Together? Yes," I said.

His head bobbed as the confirmation registered.

Cora picked up her purse from the edge of the pool table. "Excuse me. I need to powder my nose."

She'd have been better off holding it, if the ladies' smelled anything like the men's. The stink of stale piss was usually only endured by patrons wishing to powder their nose from the inside.

"She scrubs up well. I almost didn't recognise her," Matt said, watching her head bob down the corridor.

Without warning, a huge meat hook of a hand slammed onto my shoulder. "Well look who decided to show his face. Either you have a death wish or you're here to return my cash."

Fuck. In my hurry to show Cora my idea of a good time, the consequences of returning to the club hadn't even crossed my mind.

Steeling myself, I turned to face the tattooed hulk who'd spoken. "Haven't you already taken it in kind from my brother?"

His top lip curled. "Sloppy job that. They should have finished him off." A finger jabbed into my chest. "Twenty-four hours, three grand, right here, or that piece of ass," he cocked a chin towards Cora entering the bathroom, "gets to visit your grave instead of the piss pot."

Matt leaned back, bracing himself against the pool table, totally unfazed. "That sounds suspiciously like a death threat to me, mate."

"What's it to you?"

"It's against the law. Couple the threat with a GBH and you're looking at ten to life, if memory serves." He held eye contact and took a slug of his beer.

"Dumbass cops don't give a shit what goes down here."

"There's a badge in my pocket just itching to test that theory, so I suggest you leave my friend here alone, and crawl back into your den, or I'll know where to send the boys."

Tattooed Guy assessed Matt and turned to me snarling. "Fuck this bullshit. Your poxy pot and piss-ant brother ain't worth the hassle."

I let go of my breath, as he knocked my shoulder on his way past, and I watched him disappear down the same corridor as Cora had.

Matt pushed back to standing. "You never told me your brother had taken a beating. When was that?"

"Um ... a week last Tuesday."

"Why didn't you report it?"

"He's fine. It wasn't a big deal."

"Want me to ask around? Add it to our list of enquiries?"

"Nah. That's okay, dude. It's better left."

"Fair enough." Matt cocked his head in the direction Tattooed Guy had gone. "You owe that scumbag money?"

"No. I won it fair and square."

"Ah, an unlucky victim of the back room. You lose even when you win."

"You know what goes down here?"

"Sure. This club's been on our radar for months, but we're more interested in the drugs racket that your mate and his gang are running. We got a tip-off a while ago about it. I came here tonight to poke around a bit, check word hasn't got out of what's coming."

"Which is?"

"Let's just say, if all goes to plan, they won't be throwing their weight around for much longer." He placed his bottle on the wall ledge. "Take my advice and stay away from this place for a while."

Cora returned to my side. "And why would you be advising that, Matthew?"

"Health hazard," he improvised. "Too much time here, not good for the lungs, you know."

She nodded. "I do feel a little woozy."

I took that as my cue, and smacked her ass playfully. "Better get you home to bed, then."

♠ ♠ ♠

Chapter Twenty-Three

Following Matt's advice, I played it safe and stayed away from the club. Life settled into a pleasant routine, and with my leaflets generating a few more phone calls, I was kept busy most days. Cora stuck to her daily activities, and when I got the chance, between jobs, I joined her on her daily run—more for peace of mind than fitness. Letting her out of my sight became harder every day. It often turned into a race which I even let her win, occasionally. Our evenings were spent slobbing on the sofa; with me channel hopping the TV and Cora with her head nestled on my lap and her nose stuck in her latest literary find. Life was good.

I saw Kendrick only a handful of times. College term was over, and even though I had no idea how he was spending his days, he ensured me he was keeping out of trouble, and took pleasure in telling me, more than once, that being with Cora was turning me into an old man who should butt out of his business. Unless I caught wind of his desire to pursue his interest in the street racing scene, that was precisely what I intended to do.

My only worry was Pappa. He'd made it out into the garden, one cloudy day, to deadhead a few flowers, but inside the house, a layer of dust was creeping over the surfaces, and because it appeared not to bother him, it bothered me. A lot.

Everything changed when Nessie finally made an appearance.

I heard her before I saw her. The argument with her mother was louder than the electric saw I was using to cut the wood for the pergola. I downed tools and listened, undecided if I should intrude on their mother daughter reunion. Considering the decibels emitting from the kitchen, it wasn't a happy one, and if I thought Kendrick had given me an ear bashing over our relationship, it was nothing compared to the one Cora was receiving.

"It's embarrassing, Mum. It's bad enough that you've shacked up with the gardener, but he's young enough to be my brother. How would you feel if I started seeing one of Dad's friends?"

"That's hardly the same thing, Vanessa. And we're not … shacking up."

"You could have fooled me. He's here more than I am."

That part was true, even if the shacking up wasn't. I flicked the switch on the extension lead and stepped over it onto the path. My feet hit the steps two at a time, and I stopped short of the door with my fingers lingering over the handle, half of me needing to sick up for my woman, the other half imagining Nessie's nails scraping down my cheek.

"Speaking of which, I don't appreciate your disappearing without a word," Cora said.

"I needed space."

"You may be eighteen, but I still deserved to know where you were."

"I was angry."

"Clearly, your break doesn't seem to have changed that fact."

"What did you expect? You've made us the laughing stock of the neighbourhood."

"Oh, don't be so melodramatic. If people were talking, I would know."

If people weren't already talking, they would be soon. There was probably already a bunch of eager eavesdroppers gathering on the front street, popcorn at the ready.

"No, you wouldn't. You live in your own little bubble of perfection. Life exists outside of there, you know."

"I realise that, but I'm happy with my bubble, and like it or not, Johnny is part of it now. Can't you two just get along, to please me?"

"Yeah, because that's what I live for."

Cora shouldn't be spoken to like that; she deserved more respect. Nessie was being a brat. Fuck it. I had to face her sooner or later. I took a deep breath and pushed open the door. "Hello, Nessie. It's nice to see you home."

"Home? Home?" She whirled around and slammed her hand on the kitchen table. "This is not your home. This is my home. Don't think for one minute you're wheedling your money-grabbing self into this house."

I held up my hands, readying to defend from the nails. "It's not like that."

"Okay then. How is it? Tell me. I'm all ears."

"I can't explain. Your mother and I ... well ... none of it was planned. It just happened."

"Someone like you wanting someone like her doesn't just happen. There's always a motive, and the only one I can come up with is money."

Realising Nessie's aggression only came from her mouth, my hands slowly lowered. "Other than being paid for the work I do, your mother's money has never entered my mind."

"Sure, it has. I've heard the rumours."

"What rumours?"

"You're a gambler."

"So?"

"So, you're trouble."

"Since when did enjoying a game of cards make me trouble?"

"Since you got your brother beaten up."

"Says who?"

Cora laid a hand on her daughters arm. "Vanessa, what are you saying?"

"Mum, you have to get rid of him. He's bad news."

Where did Nessie get off, lumping me in with the troublemakers in town? I had no desire to cause Cora any more stress, but I had to defend myself. "You've got it all wrong. I haven't done anything." I hoped.

"Oh, really. That's not what I heard."

"Yeah? What exactly have you heard?"

"Do I have to spell it out?"

"Actually ... yes."

"Fine. Jess's friend, Lisa, is friends with another girl called Yvonne, and her boyfriend, Rhys, hangs around the racing scene with Barbie. Apparently, Barbie doesn't like your brother too much, since he started spending time with his girl."

Geez, did she ever take a breath? "Wait. Barbie's a guy?"

"Of course, Barbie's a guy. Are you not listening? Chris Barber, he's called. Anyway, Barbie thinks Molly is getting too cosy with Rick. That's your brother, right?"

Where the hell was she going with this? "Um, yeah."

"Well Lisa thinks Molly just felt sorry for Rick when he got a pasting on account of your stirring up shit with the Schofield brothers."

"Who are they?"

"Don't play the innocent. Everyone knows the Schofield brothers, even me."

"I've got to say you have me at a disadvantage."

"I can't see how. You were the one fleecing them at poker." She paused with her head cocked to one side and her lips pursed, as I mentally pictured the men around the card table and tried to deduce which of them could be related. "Two guys, loads of tattoos, one of them a big snake. Remember now?" Her eyebrows rose and stayed there.

"Ah."

"Johnny? Is this true?" Cora asked.

"It was no big deal. Two small games for some extra cash. I knew when to get out. Honestly, I haven't been back since." I cupped Cora's shoulders in my hands. "Baby, this has nothing to do with us. Why are you listening to idle gossip?"

Little crinkles marred the bridge of Cora's nose. "I saw a man of that description, when we went to your club."

Nessie gasped. "You took my mother to the Pocket Scratcher?"

"So what?"

"Everyone knows what goes on in that dive. I suppose the next thing you're going to tell me is that you scored her a hit and you both got high together."

"Don't be an idiot." I regretted the words as soon as I spoke them. Nessie was determined to paint me as the villain, and I was playing right into her hands. Cora pulled away from me and stood staring at her fingers stroking over the counter top. "Cora, look at me."

Her fingers changed rhythm and began tapping a new pattern into the work surface. "Go home, Johnny."

Where did that come from? "I'm sorry?"

"I need to think."

"What about?"

"Us. Gambling is one thing, but violence and drugs ... I had no idea you were associated with any of that."

"I'm not."

"Go. Please."

"No. I'm not going anywhere."

"Vanessa's right. We were naïve to think this would work. I can't be with another man hiding secrets."

"I don't have secrets. Sure I've got into a few fights. Who hasn't? And I admit I've tried weed, once, about five years ago, but I'm nothing like Nessie is trying to make me out to be. Ask me anything. I'll tell you everything you want to know."

Nessie stepped so close to me I could feel her anger radiating from her body. "Everything she wants to hear, you mean."

"I have never lied to your mother. I made a promise to her that I never would, and I've kept that promise. Cora ..."

"She asked you to go. What are you still doing here?" Nessie smiled smugly.

"Get out of my face, Nessie. You've done enough damage. Cora, please ..."

Cora's head was shaking. "Don't you see? You lied to me by omission."

"There's a bunch of stuff you don't know about me yet. Neither of us came with a freaking manual."

"If this conversation is a sample page, I don't want to read anymore. We were basing a relationship on physical feelings, chasing a dream. It's a fantasy to think otherwise."

"It isn't a dream; it's real. I felt it; you felt it. No one knows everything about each other when they first start out, but we'll learn."

"No. I don't think I want to. Everything's against us, there's so much animosity, and now this. I can't do it."

"I know it's hard, but I promise I'm not the bad guy in this, and everyone will come to accept us, eventually. You have to keep fighting, Cora. Don't give up on me, please."

"My head is all jumbled up. I need to be alone, Johnny."

I moved to stand behind her and spoke into her hair. "You don't mean that."

Her body stiffened. "Please Johnny."

It was as if a screen had been drawn between us, locking me out, and keeping me out until she said the word. I breathed in the unmistakable aroma of the scent I'd become so used to being around, wondering if it would be the last time I ever smelt it. Cora was angry, confused. She didn't know what she was saying. Sure, she wanted me gone, now, but tomorrow she would realise how stupid she was being. "Fine," I said. "If it's what you want, I'll leave, as long as you understand it's not what I want, and I'll be back. Just let me know when you're ready, and I'll be here. I haven't given up on us, even if you have."

Nessie grabbed my arm and spun me towards the door. "I guess that's you done then. You'll see this is the right thing to do." She opened the door and pushed me through it. "Bye now."

I stared at the combination of frosted glass and UPVC, unable to digest what had just taken place. I'd gone up against a slip of a girl, and lost. I should have known better than to try to come between mother and daughter, but I refused to believe I'd lost Cora. It wasn't possible. Relationships sucked.

♠ ♠ ♠

Chapter Twenty-Four

With an anvil tied to my heart, I gathered up my tools, shoved them into my holdall, and took a farewell look at the pergola. I hated to leave a job unfinished; this one more than any. I'd poured my heart and soul into the design and construction, needing to get it absolutely right for the woman I loved—every curve, every nail placed with precision, to ensure the finished result would be as perfect as she was.

"I haven't finished with you," I said to the structure, before hitching my bag onto my shoulder and leaving it behind.

At home, the house was quiet, too quiet.

"Pappa. Paps!" The only answer I received was a bark from Smokey. At least someone was still speaking to me. The barking continued, but Smokey didn't appear. It was coming from upstairs. I guessed the faithful hound was accompanying Pappa on his afternoon nap, and if he didn't zip it soon, he'd wake Pappa up, and then somehow it would become my fault that Paps was cranky for the rest of the day.

I dumped my bag on the hallway floor, kicked off my shoes, and climbed the stairs. "Smokey, quiet, boy. Shh. Give the old man some peace."

Smokey's head turned as I pushed open the door.

"Come on, boy. Out of there," I shouted in a husky whisper, cocking my head for him to follow me.

He whimpered and laid his chin on the edge of the bed, with his big, black eyes focused on Pappa's face.

"I said, come on." I pursed my lips and tried to squeeze a silent whistle from them, but Smokey was playing at being deaf. Sighing, I walked over and tugged on his collar, but it was as if he were stuck to the floor. Damn, he was being a stubborn bastard. "All right then, stay, but quit with the noise," I said through gritted teeth.

I'd had a shitty afternoon, and I didn't have any fight left in me to waste on stupid doggy games. All I wanted to do was kick back a bucket load of beers and pass out.

As soon as I tried to leave, the barking started up again.

I shot back to Smokey's side. "What the fuck is up with you, today?" His behaviour was driving me nuts.

Smokey stood and nudged Pappa's hand.

"What is it, boy?"

I studied Pappa, his pale face looking even more washed-out against the white of the sheets. His mouth hung open but no snoring could be heard. Smokey licked Pappa's hand and looked at me.

A sudden coldness, shivered through me, and my body couldn't move. My eyes scanned from Pappa's face to his chest, praying I'd see even the slightest of rise and falls. As the seconds ticked by, I stared, not breathing, but saw nothing.

No. Please, God, no. Not this. Not now. Not today. I wasn't ready. Pappa wasn't ready. He had to be fine. When I'd left him this morning, we'd discussed my room. He'd been happy to allow me to redecorate, even offered to help. He couldn't be ...

Smokey let out a small whine and nudged Pappa's hand again, stirring me from my stupor. I reached for Pappa's wrist, hoping to find a beat under his tissue paper skin, but it was cold and still.

My hand shot to my forehead. Think, Johnny, think. I couldn't think. An incessant pounding had invaded my skull and wiped out any remaining brainpower. Then without consciously doing so, I pulled my phone from my back pocket and dialled the emergency services.

"I think my grandfather is dead."

In a matter of minutes, someone had squeezed out every last bit of joy from my heart, taken the rock that remained, and smashed it with a sledgehammer. I backed against the wall, slid down it, and slumped on the floor, cradling my head in my hands. Time slowed and became meaningless. Nothing mattered anymore.

I barely registered the arrival of the doctor. His words washed over me, and I watched trance-like as my grandfather's body was taken from his beloved home.

Kendrick arrived as the vehicle pulled away. His eyes followed it down the road. "What's going on? Who was that? What were they doing here?"

"Paps."

"Paps? What do you mean, Paps? Where is he?"

I nodded at the vehicle as it turned the corner.

"He was in there? Is he okay?"

I shook my head silently and turned to re-enter the house.

"What's going on?" Kendrick asked, following me. "Speak to me, man." He grabbed my arm, forcing me to face him.

I pushed the words from my mouth and told him everything.

He stilled. "Shit." Collapsing onto the sofa, he looked at me. "That sucks. What are we going to do?"

"I don't know."

"Will we have to move?"

"I don't know."

"Where will we go?"

"I don't know. Just quit the questions, will you?"

♠ ♠ ♠
Chapter Twenty-Five

I slept through most of the next day, and the next. I didn't see any point in getting up, until a musty odour threatened to wilt the flowers on the wallpaper. Finally surfacing, I bunged my sheets in the washing machine and ate my first meal, but I still wasn't ready to face the world. All I wanted was to reach out and seek comfort in Cora's arms.

My brain got stuck on standby, and days turned to a week without my noticing. Retreating into myself and sticking to routine somehow kept me numb, and meant I didn't have to think anymore. Not once leaving the house, I left the phone unanswered and only opened my mouth to bark at Kendrick when he attempted conversation. Even Smokey gave up trying to attract my attention and barely acknowledged my presence when I walked into the room. I knew I should take him for his walks—his stomach grew rounder by the day on a diet of stale dog biscuits and leftover takeout—but the front door felt like the hatch of a submerged submarine I daren't open for fear of the world crashing through and drowning any remaining life left in me. Most of my time was spent sitting in Pappa's chair, staring at the floor. The house wasn't the same without the sound of coughing reverberating around the walls, or the scent of tobacco hanging in the air.

How quickly my life had turned to shit. This wasn't how things were supposed to happen. Nothing that had occurred, since I'd returned from uni, had been part of my plan for the future. A small part of my brain knew I had to get back on track, but it wasn't strong enough to kick-start the rest of it into action. It was as if I were driving along a country road with no street lighting and broken headlights, and I couldn't see a way out of the darkness.

With the arrival of a new week, the numbness faded and my brain slowly reengaged. I realised Pappa's body wouldn't be held indefinitely, and I had to start making plans, whether I was ready to or not. But where to begin?

I should have been used to funerals, but my parents had both been cremated, and their spirits now drifted over their favourite picnic spot by the river, where I'd scattered their ashes. I had no idea what Pappa's wishes were. Back when Gran was alive, they'd been churchgoers, but I was clueless as to whether Pappa wanted to be buried in St Mark's, or not. Besides, Gran was on the mantelpiece.

My eyes drifted from the ornate urn to the bureau, beside Pappa's chair, and a tear pooled as I remembered him sitting in front of it, glasses balanced on the end of his nose, pen in hand. He kept everything of importance behind that wooden slope. I reached over and pulled down the lid. A piece of paper drifted from within and landed at my feet; it was an electric bill. Had it been paid? Pappa had never entered the twenty-first century and bought a computer, but had he, at least, joined the twentieth to set up direct debits? What about his bank account? There was so much to think about and organise, it made my head spin. I riffled through more piles of paperwork and dragged a couple of folders from the back of the bureau to make a start.

An hour later, I had a pile of payment demands, bank statements, an address book, birth and marriage certificates, and a business card with the name of a solicitor embossed across the middle. Underneath were the words, Divorce, Employment, and Probate Specialist. It was my only lead, so I made a call, and struck lucky.

The following day, Kendrick and I sat nervously in the solicitor's office as he read through Pappa's will. His property was to be split equally between Kendrick and myself. My surprise was short-lived. Unless Pappa had left everything to the dog's home, there really wasn't anyone else in the picture. And although I was relieved we wouldn't have to up sticks, I would rather have had Pappa back than any amount of inheritance. The solicitor talked us through the normal procedure, and the things I should prioritise, and by the time we left, my head was much straighter, despite my heart being in pieces.

With so much to do, life became a series of daily tasks to be carried out, but when I managed them, I could fool myself into thinking everything was going to be okay. And with each one I completed, my head became a little clearer.

I thought about Cora every day. Every time I closed my eyes, I saw her. Every time I heard the clattering of a dustbin lid, I ran to the window, hoping to catch a glimpse of her. I wondered what she was doing, how she was feeling, and whether she was thinking about me, too. Did she even know about Pappa? Would she want to know? Should I call round to tell her? It would give me an excuse to see her. I wanted to give her the space she'd asked for, even though the wait was agonising. But it wasn't the time to fight for Cora's affections; I already had more than I could deal with.

The funeral passed by without a hitch. Pappa was laid to rest, in the plot he'd reserved, under the sycamore tree at St Mark's, cradling Gran's ashes to his chest. Afterwards, everyone congregated in the local community centre, where Pappa's gardening club had organised a wake.

Standing amongst a group of strangers swapping stories of Pappa's plant propagating prowess was low on my entertainment list, and I didn't have a speck of inclination to push it any higher. I couldn't wait to get it over with.

"Johnny, isn't it?" An elderly gentleman appeared at my side.

Why can't everyone just leave me the fuck alone? I sighed. "Yeah. That's right."

"My condolences to you and your brother. Your grandfather was a good man. We'll miss him at the Rotary."

"Thank you. We'll miss him too," I said, forcing a smile. I'd lost count of the number of times I'd said those words in one day, and it was beginning to grate on my nerves.

"Ron taught my grandaughter everything she knows about geraniums, didn't he, Paige?" The old man stepped to the side, revealing a pretty, but petite, girl, wearing a high-necked dress and flat shoes. She couldn't have been more than nineteen.

The girl nodded her head. The long, auburn fringe, of her otherwise closely cropped hair, fell across her sharp cheekbones, and cloaked one hazel eye. "He was a sweet man," she said, sweeping the hair back with her hand. "Do you know much about geraniums?"

"A little," I answered, not wishing to appear a know-it-all. She was kinda cute, if you liked the waif look. Before I met Cora, I probably would have asked for her number, but as much as Paige was batting her eyelashes at me, it was having no effect. All I could think about was Cora. I'd fallen hard. She had me, body and soul, and I couldn't imagine being with anyone else.

"You don't share your grandfather's passion for flowers then?" she asked.

"I prefer bushes."

Her eyes twinkled. "You do?"

"Yeah. Give me a lush privet hedge to clip into shape and I'm in my element."

"I'm down with that." She smiled.

Paige's flirting felt alien to me. I hadn't meant for her to read anything into my words, so I stared at my feet, hoping she'd get the message that I wasn't interested. "I'll bear that in mind."

"Paige? Are you Ready to go?"

My gaze rose at the sound of her grandfather's gravelly voice.

A wrinkled hand wrapped around Paige's elbow. "Well actually ..." she started.

"Nice to meet you, Paige," I interrupted. "Keep watering the geraniums." I felt bad dismissing her, but better that than leading her on.

I turned from the pair and stopped dead in my tracks, unsure if I were hallucinating.

"Hello Johnny."

♠ ♠ ♠

Chapter Twenty-Six

My mood lifted immediately and my mouth opened, but everything I wanted to say got tangled in my throat.

"I'm so sorry about Ronald," she said. Somehow, I didn't mind hearing the sentiment from her lips. "I would have come to see you sooner, but I only heard this morning."

I watched her lips move as she spoke, and all I could think about was tasting them again. My hands twitched at my sides, eager to reach out and touch places I knew so well. "You would?"

"Naturally. He was my friend. I've known him for years. I feel awful that he died and I didn't even know about it. What kind of neighbour does that make me?"

The elation I felt at her appearance suddenly evaporated. "Don't worry about it." I sighed. As usual, Cora was thinking of formalities.

"How are you?"

And yet? "Pretty shit."

She nodded. "And Kendrick."

"He's okay, I guess."

"It must have been terrible for you."

Now she cared? "It was. I found him right after you threw me out of your house," I said with a note of bitterness.

"Oh Johnny, that's awful. I'm so sorry."

"You've said that."

"It's true."

"Is it?" How could she leave me hanging for a couple of weeks and then turn up out of the blue, acting as if nothing more than propriety had led her back to me?

"Of course, it is. What do you take me for?"

I leaned in, a little too close, and simmering anger threw me in her face. "What exactly are you sorry for? Pappa dying? Throwing me out? Or believing your daughter's lies about me?" As soon as I said the words, I regretted them.

Cora glanced over my shoulder, and her eyes surveyed the room. "Please don't shout at me, Johnny. You're causing a scene."

I placed my hand loosely around her waist and steered her into a corner, away from the majority of mourners. "I'm sorry, but this isn't exactly how I'd pictured us meeting up again."

"No. Me neither."

"So, you have pictured it?"

"I've had a lot to think about, in the past couple of weeks."

"Us?"

"Yes."

"And?"

"I miss you." She paused. "But …"

"Why does there always have to be a 'but' with you? Can't you just say you miss me, and leave it at that? I miss you is great. I miss you, I can do something about. Christ, Cora, you've no idea what I've been going through. You have to come back to me."

"I thought we agreed."

"Agreed what? I didn't agree to anything. You told me to leave. I didn't want to go, but you needed space. That's all I've done, given you space. I wasn't finished with our relationship. I'm still not."

"But …"

"Another but?"

"You don't have children. You wouldn't understand."

"Try me anyway."

"I want to be a good mother. And Vanessa—"

"Isn't a kid anymore. Like you said, she'll be away to university soon, and then who knows where. You've been a good mother, but that part of your life is gone. You have to move on." I pulled her close. My hand pressed against her back, sealing the contact, and her breasts squeezed

201

tightly against my chest. Her scent wrapped around me, and her arms felt like home. It was impossible to stay mad with her. "It's time for you. And me." I dipped my head into her shoulder, and couldn't resist laying a soft kiss on her collarbone.

She let out a small gasp. "Johnny. Stop. Please. People are watching."

"Let them." The feel of her brought everything back, and I didn't care who saw.

She tried to part from my arms. "I have to go."

I increased my hold. No way was I letting her get away from me again. "Good idea. I'll come with you. We need to continue this conversation."

"The host can't leave."

"Good job it's not my gig, then," I said, grabbing her hand and pulling her towards the door.

As I turned to go through it, Kendrick blocked my path. "Where are you two sneaking off to?" he asked, his eyes flicking between Cora and me.

"Home."

"Not without me, you don't," he said. I needed some alone time with Cora and opened my mouth to say so, but before I could utter a word, he continued, "Don't worry. I won't cramp your style. Just get me out of here. I can't stand spending another minute with these old fogies." He grinned at Cora. "I don't think we've been introduced."

Cora smiled back. "Kendrick, isn't it?"

"Call me Rick."

"Hello Rick."

I pushed through the door. "Introductions can wait. Let's go."

❀ ❀ ❀

I followed Cora back to Parkside Avenue and dropped Kendrick off at the house. But before returning to Cora, I needed to get something.

"What the fuck are you doing?" Kendrick asked, holding on to the banister as I strode up the stairs. He was still waiting for an answer when I ran back down with the tiny box in my hand. "What's that you've got there?" he asked suspiciously.

I flipped the lid as I passed.

Rick's mouth gaped at the sight of the glistening rock. "Shit, dude. That's Mum's ring. You serious?"

"Never more so," I said, breathless.

"Damn it, Bro, that's some heavy shit."

"Sure is."

"Aren't you rushing things?" he shouted, as I dashed out the door.

Maybe I was, but I needed Cora to understand I wasn't some kid, that this was it for me. She was it.

By the time I'd sprinted over the garden, to next-door, Cora was inside, and her door was locked. I banged my fist against it.

"Cora! Cora!" Why wasn't she answering? "Cora!"

Her voice filtered through the woodwork. "Do you have to make so much noise?"

"Open the damn door and I won't have to."

"I think it better if I don't."

"Better for who? Not better for me. I'm a mess without you. Do you know how many times I've walked around the garden, hoping to catch a glimpse of you through the window? Or how many nights I've lain in my bed, imagining you lying next to me? Kendrick even talked about getting me committed. If you want to see me in the crazy house, you're off to a good start. If not, let me in so we can talk about this."

"I'm afraid if I let you in, I won't be able to let you go."

"Great! I'm good with that. Come on, Cora. Take the risk. I am not having this conversation through a slab of wood, with the neighbour's curtains twitching." I paused, listening for any sign of movement. As each second passed, anxiety turned to anger. "Open the door, Cora. Open the fucking door, or I'll break it down."

A whisper filtered through the cracks. "I believe you would too."

"Damn right, I would."

The lock clicked, and the door slowly opened. I was in. It was all I needed, time alone with Cora, with no one sticking their face in our business.

She turned her back on me, and walked into the living room. "I had coffee with Sheila this morning."

Small talk? Really? "Oh?"

"Yes. It was Sheila who told me about Ronald."

"I'm not here to talk about Pappa."

Cora curled onto the sofa and hooked her hands under her legs. "She told me something else too."

I sat down beside her, laying my arm along the cushion next to her head. My lips were inches from hers, and burned with the desire to taste them. "I'm not interested in gossip. I want to talk about us."

Her eyes lowered. "You might find what she had to say interesting."

"Unless she told you what a fool you were to let me go, and to hightail your ass back to me, I doubt it."

"Actually, she was talking about visiting her son at the hospital."

"Matt? Is he all right?"

"He was shot in a raid."

"Fuck. But he's alive?"

"Yes. The bullet missed his major organs. He was very lucky. Another officer died."

"That sucks. Glad Matt's okay, though. Can we get back to the subject of us now?" My hand unconsciously drifted to her shoulder, and I smoothed the back of my fingers over her skin.

She froze but didn't shrug me away. "Matthew had a message for you."

"What message?"

"He wanted you to know that it turns out the Schofield brothers were out of town on the day you mentioned."

"Out of town?"

"Securing a shipment of drugs, it seems." Slowly her eyes met mine. "So you see they couldn't have hurt your brother."

"I guess not." *So who the fuck had?*

"You weren't to blame, Johnny."

Although secretly relieved to learn that Kendrick's beating wasn't my fault, after all, I wasn't about to admit my long held fears that it probably was, and I was still pissed at Cora's readiness to lay the blame at my door. "And saying that makes everything okay, does it?"

"I didn't want to believe the worst."

My fingers stilled and the tips pressed into her flesh. "Didn't stop you, though."

"I'm sorry I misjudged you. I told you I needed time to think."

"You've had time."

"Yes."

"And?"

"It was hard. I thought I'd decided, but I've been thinking about what you said at the wake."

"Which bit?"

"Vanessa."

"And?"

"You're right. It doesn't seem to matter how much I try with her. I'm losing my grip. She doesn't need me anymore. It's time I accepted that fact."

"You'll always be her mother, and a girl always needs her mum. But you're a woman too. One with needs of her own."

She nodded. "I am. But I need to know you're committed to us. I don't want to be hurt again."

Hearing the word hurt made me realise how firmly I was gripping her shoulder. I relaxed and let my hand fall to hers. "I'm committed. I'm so committed. Just let me prove it to you."

"You're really ready for this?"

"I'm ready." How many times did I have to say it? "From the moment I met you, there has been no one else in my bed or on my mind. You got into my head and refused to leave. Your beauty and poise captured my heart. Sure, sometimes you frustrate the hell out of me, but I enjoy a challenge."

"You enjoy a challenge?"

"Yeah."

Cora inhaled deeply through her nose. "What if I said I was pregnant?" It came so out of the blue, it took me a second to answer.

"I'd say condoms are shit."

"I'm serious. What would you say?" The way she held my gaze, tiny grooves forming between her brows, told me I had to choose my words carefully. The woman sure knew how to mind-fuck.

"Are you?"

"Answer the question, Johnny."

Squeezing the square lump in my trouser pocket, with my free hand, I tested the waters. "I'd ask you to marry me."

The grooves deepened. "Why?"

"Because I want to take care of you."

"You do?"

"Yeah. Baby or no baby." I paused. "Is there a baby?" I asked, heart pounding.

Her lips curled at the corners. "No."

"Christ, Cora. That's not funny."

An evil smile plumped out her cheeks. "Your face was."

"You're a sick woman. You know that? Underneath your prim and proper exterior lies a wicked centre I can't wait to see a whole lot more of."

Cora was still smiling, as my words washed over her. "You want to marry me?"

I thought about the ring in my pocket. We didn't need to rush things. Cora would wear it someday. "Someday."

"Ah … someday."

"Yes." I pulled her close. Her breath was warm against my neck. "But until then, please say I can finally call you mine?"

"On one condition."

"What's that?"

"No more gambling."

"I can run with that. So we have a deal?"

"We do."

"Promise?"

"I love you."

"Love?"

"I said that, didn't I?"

I always thought I'd be the one to say the words first, but she'd beaten me to it, and I couldn't have been happier. "You did."

"Then I must have meant it."

"I love you too."

When the time was right, I'd ask the question, but for now, we had each other, and that was all I needed.

THE END

AKNOWLEDGEMENTS

I would like to say thank you to all the people who helped make this book possible; your patience, support, and technical knowledge have been invaluable.

7183444R00124

Printed in Great Britain
by Amazon.co.uk, Ltd.,
Marston Gate.